THE HOP QUAD DOLLY

For Susie.
And, of course, Button.

THE HOP QUAD DOLLY

Simon Carr

Hutchinson
LONDON SYDNEY AUCKLAND JOHANNESBURG

This edition first published in 1991 by
Hutchinson

Random Century Group Ltd
20 Vauxhall Bridge Road, London SW1V 2SA

Random Century Australia (Pty) Ltd
20 Alfred Street, Milsons Point, Sydney, NSW 2061, Australia

Random Century New Zealand Ltd
PO Box 40–086, Glenfield, Auckland 10, New Zealand

Random Century South Africa (Pty) Ltd
PO Box 337, Bergvlei, 2012, South Africa

British Library Cataloguing in Publication Data
Carr, Simon *1952–*
The hop quad dolly.
I. Title
823.914 [F]

ISBN 0–09–174830–5

Photoset by Deltatype Ltd, Ellesmere Port, Cheshire
Printed and bound in Great Britain by
Mackays of Chatham PLC, Chatham, Kent

Author's Remarks

This is a public school story. It happens to be my story but it's no different from any other. We all know it, and have come, I dare say, to love it.

Everything you've ever enjoyed in a public school story is here. A familiar gallery of schoolboys, scholars and sporting heroes. There is a fight, and comic foreigner. There is a stolen postal order. There is a terrific flogging in the middle. There is an overwhelming try scored in the last few pages, and everything ends – as far as anything ends happily – happily.

A major public school story, you see. Deep stairwells. Concave steps. Oak doors with iron studs. Stone corridors wide enough to take a gun carriage.

You'll like it. Sort of thing you can read in bed. Nice short chapters. I know what you want. You're in safe hands now.

An anachronism, you say? How would you like a punch on the snout

People complain about housing conditions, don't they?

My father lived for a month in a water buffalo.

He was logging troop movements in the Hindu Kush. Enemy activity had been reported, so there he was. Very, very cold indeed up there, with the temperature and so forth. Look into the wind and your eyeballs freeze. Then they burst. The poor man was freezing to death. He was opening a tin of beef and one of his fingers broke off.

So, when he was hiding in a defile and saw a water buffalo trapped on its back, he killed it. He couldn't help wondering what the poor brute was doing so far out of its natural habitat. Much the same as himself, he thought, as the Swiss Army penknife did its awful work.

But, you know, when he managed to remove enough material from the beast to crawl inside he found it wonderful accommodation. Cosy, you know? Snug quarters. Get used to anything if you have to. *That's* the value of a public school education.

I live in Albany myself. I've got used to it. No normal person would put up with it. My rooms sit above a successful psychotherapist and below a popular drug addict (I assume he's a drug addict). But we rub along pretty well. Because, you understand, I have seen the world.

You want to know what I look like?

You will want to know what I look like. That's fair enough. I'm not one to bang on about these things, but I've got an Irish tweed suit, get the picture? You'd know me if you saw me. Come and have a glass of pop. Bring your sister. We'll go punting. I'll run you up to Oxford in the Bentley. I was at Oxford, of course. Long shadows across the wicket. Girls in summer dresses. Before the war, whichever war it was. Or was it Cambridge? One or the other, you'd know me if you saw me.

Thursdays I sit in Kettners. Always have done, I don't know why. What I do know is that Philip VI of Spain died of heat flushes because the servant in charge of the brazier couldn't be located to move the brazier, so they didn't move it, and the king died as a result.

I like that.

It's the least I can do, in my own small way, to stick by my guns and contribute *something* to the stability of this rapidly changing world.

Thus, every Thursday I sit in Kettners. I don't like it very much, but then I never did. Been getting very grimy over the last 25 years. Full of service industry types. Fashion stylists. Catwalk sluts. Scissormen and mirror-men. I saw a man there once with a ponytail, what do you think of that? In happier times the bar was full of demi-debs plotting against their rivals. Painters' models. One or two virtually naked women. I like all that sort of thing, there's nothing funny about me. There were writers too, wearing Irish tweed suits. I always wanted to be a writer, but that's enough about that.

So where does it all begin?

On Waterloo station in the gathering dusk.

An affecting sight: brave little boy sitting on a tuckbox. His mother long gone. ('You don't mind if I don't wait, darling, I so hate goodbyes.') His feet scarcely touched the twentieth century – the cigarette boxes and used contraceptives that litter the platform.

Such boys interest me. I questioned him closely. I discovered he was waiting for a train to take him – by a micropolitan coincidence – to his first term at my old school.

His first day! His first term!

Lord, can you remember that first day of your first term at your public school? The smell of that crisp autumn morning as you sailed down the drive and saw the rugger posts up on XX Acre? The trunks coming in across the quadrangles, every wall thick with ivy, the deciduous trees tinged with a fringe of nicotine. Remember the gaslight in Half Quad, the medieval bells, the ravens hopping across the lawns. The sharp linen in the new bed, the mist drifting down the clock tower and through the courts.

'You paint a pretty picture, sir,' he said, and haltingly he started to ventilate his own small hopes and fears.

'Yes, yes, yes,' I agreed with him quickly. 'It can be a lonely business, your first term at an English public school. A shrivelling business indeed.' I saw the lad pale and his fingers tense around his thin little knees, so I hastened to reassure him. 'But buck up! It's a great adventure too. My nephew tells me the first day of term is full of bustle and colour. It's like a train station, that's how he describes it. Exactly! I told him. That's exactly how I found it myself. Like a train station. In Warsaw. In 1939, and the Axis artillery is opening up and your grandmother's name is Levi!'

I was hooting, but the little chin was beginning to buckle, he wasn't getting the hang of this at all. 'No, no, but you young shavers – the camaraderie between you! The deep and abiding friendships! You can't imagine how quickly you bond with your fellows when you're bundled in a laundry skip together and pitched down a stairwell.

And you're a good looking little tyke, too – don't smile too bright at the Captain of Swimming!'

'And beating sir?' he asked. 'Do they beat you very often?'

'Oh, rarely – very rarely – I can scarcely *remember* going to bed without being beaten, if only by the Captain of Swimming when the Bloods were drunk!'

'I daresay it has changed a good deal since your day, sir,' my young friend offered with a hopeful expression on his face.

'It went the wrong way there for a while, you're right. But don't you believe it now. It's all coming back again, you know. By George, I can feel it in the breaks of my bones!'

I packed him off with a sixpenny bit and a clout round the ear, but I was not half so cheerful as I was letting on. As soon as he had gone, a melancholy took me . . . The dusk, the dusk, the gathering shadows. Defeated commuters in their drab stuff suits. The yellow flare of sodium lights in a halo of lead poisoning. The drizzle collects, and the nights draw in. Autumn leaves scuttle across the Mall. The century is coming to an end. There is a millenial chill in the air.

Now where were we?

We were at Salisbury College, if it's any of your damn business!

Oh excuse me. I do apologise. Send me the bill for the dry cleaning. I thought you were asking where we were at school. Never ask a man where he went to school. If it was worse than yours you feel this, if it was better than yours you feel that, and where's the good in either?

So don't say anything else. Come with me. I'll hold your hand.

Suit yourself, suit yourself. I was thinking you'd be

nervous on your own. I don't want to hold *your* hand, for heaven's sake, I thought *you* might want to hold *mine*. Never mind. Let's go across these bracken fields. We'll go by the water meadows. We'll go along the Roman boundaries and over the rise with the cornflowers, and the wild daisies, and those yellow flowers with the blue petals that people like. And as we break over the rise we will see, laid out like a miniature city, Salisbury College.

Like most ancient institutions, Salisbury College is a mess. Packed together over the millenia, covered with ivy and connected by alleyways. Older than Winchester, far older than Eton, it's the oldest thing in England. So old it may always have been there.

In the centre of the school are stones standing in a circle. That's how old it is. This is pre-pyramids we're talking about. The history of those years was recorded in a language lost to us now. A language whose letters were pebbles and whose syntax was string.

Even in my time, every boy was still required to carry a phrase of this language, a length of string with three pebbles knotted in it at given distances. It was a lot of foolery I dare say, but we carried it as part of our Cozens, to be produced on demand by senior boys. The phrase was a curse against early counter-inhabitants of the marshes. '!@&*% the Beaker People!' the string was assumed to have meant. It was not a word I used myself, so I removed the offending stone and was frequently, though not painfully, beaten for it.

We learned our history carefully when I was young, but time is a cruel mistress. As is claret. Let me tell you what I can remember. I had all this at my fingertips once. I could have told you the nicknames of the assistant masters' sons during the Napoleonic wars. But what can I tell you now? Pass the brandy.

Salisbury was a singing school before the Romans came. We must have turned Christian afterwards because the Master had the power to excommunicate you. Yes, he could expel you, then excommunicate you. Then he could have you hanged. And then he could have you sent – not to

Magdalen College to take up your Exhibition – but to hell, where you would roast on a griddle for eternity. Discipline was stricter in those days.

The Christians tried to suppress the pagan elements of the school, but do you know, they couldn't. We already had roots deep in the mistletoe. An episcopal headmaster appointed from Rome came to Salisbury, went native, and was later defrocked. They had discovered him circumcising his pupils with a golden sickle in a secret druidic ceremony. Britain's first school scandal combined doubtful hygiene with religious malpractice. Salisbury enjoyed a nonconformist reputation for the next two thousand years, if memory serves.

Two thousand years is long. Life is short, but two thousand years is not. Let me condense it for you as far as I decently can.

The school's fortunes went up and down with the tide. You might plot our fortunes by the amount of building in any one era. We had been clever with the Druids, but little remains of that. There were the stones at the heart of the College, but only Lodge members were allowed to refer to them by name, let alone to see them. As a sometime Lodge member I can tell you they looked secretive. And quiet. I can say that much. Dark and quiet, and built by Druids. But already I have said too much.

We were popular with the Romans (we had a wall of theirs). The Dark Ages were neither here nor there (a couple of kings, and a coronation). But William the Conqueror took a shine to us, and in the twelfth century a Crusading party of our masters rode from Salisbury to Istanbul on College-owned land. They drank, as was their right, a cubic foot of wine per man at every inn along the way. They never came back. During the Perpendicular years we had but seven pupils, all under ten years of age, reading dog Latin without any supervision at all. The new masters drank away the Hundred Years War entirely, and the College buildings were used as the largest corn exchange in England.

The Tudors liked us and we liked them. The Stuarts

were dubious. The Hanoverians could make neither head nor tail of us, and that began to tell. We made up a rude rhyme about Queen Victoria's wedding night, which was a mistake. By the middle of her reign we were failing to attract what is now known as investment. From 1850 there was no new building whatsoever. No faux-Gothic, redbrick-with-diagonal-pattern facades, no neo-Classical whitewash, no concrete corridors, no asylum arches, no terminus vaulting. Oh give me pause to wipe away my tears of shame.

The other happy consequence of Victoria's feelings about us was this: we evaded the reforming zeal of Dr Arnold of Rugby who delivered the public school system into a greater servitude than five thousand years of school life had ever known. Arnold, you may know, was the thoroughly progressive swine who destroyed Rugby. He was a totalitarian madman who smashed the power of boys to govern themselves. He pressed prefects into a sophisticated espionage system, and sent 'lewd or loathsome boys' out into Society with a mark of Cain on the foreheads to die out East, or throw themselves off Hammersmith Bridge (a fairly awful part of town even then).

Like most revolutionaries, Arnold wanted charity. Many boys are lewd, and most are loathsome. Expel the lewd and loathsome, and who will you have in school?

We had nothing to do with Dr Arnold. Which, apart from anything else, is why we were so extremely bad at rugby football. This is by the way.

Salisbury College is a principality of domes and arches. Gables overhang alleyways. Faces look out of windows and say, 'You sir! What's your name!' There are gargoyles and so forth. It's like a city, and a forbidding city at that. But when the evening sun comes in across the college, the old stone glows.

I like that.

The buildings cover twenty-five acres. There are fine public places with courts, and quads, and flogging blocks. There is the trading quarter. There are sporting courts, and halls, and hanging galleries and hidden gardens. Cloisters and colonnades, small doors and porticos. Got its monuments. Got its slums. Got its red light district too, perhaps, but I can't tell you anything about that.

You wouldn't want to step off your path. You could easily get lost with unpleasant – unimaginable – results. Look: there is a dazed tug found by the Nightwatch underneath a buttress, out of bounds. When he rises, as he does with difficulty, he finds he is naked but for an execution shift and a Benedictine cowl over his head. As he tries to move he finds he has an apple in his arse. No, look closer – *not that close!*, let's not get morbid – it is not an apple. *It is a potato!* The boy's eyes are wide. His nostrils flare like a terrified colt. He has seen more than he should, for a boy his age, but if you say he didn't deserve it you don't know what you're talking about.

This is a story, it has to be said, with moments of sudden violence. And I am aware of a bourgeois prejudice against violence among elements of literate society. They don't like it. They write letters to the press about it. So we must first address the question in a forthright sort of way: tidy the matter up in order to proceed on a sound footing.

But the violence in schools today is dreadful, is it not?

Indeed, indeed, you hear a lot about the violence in schools these days. It excites the Wimbledon voter. Nothing wrong with that. It's what the Wimbledon voter is for: to cancel his subscription to magazines, and write letters to the press on the subject of violence in schools.

But this may surprise you: it is not just Wimbledon that feels like this. Expert pollsters have determined – by a statistical anomaly – that 108 per cent of the poll-sensitive population believes that there should be less violence in schools.

This may surprise you even more: I agree!

For instance: I am wholly – not to say fiercely – opposed to teachers carrying knives in class. I will speak out against this at public meetings. I will write letters to the *Daily Mail*. I will cancel my subscription to the *Spectator*. I will not be silent on this point.

But goodness knows I am sympathetic to a fault to the pupil who chooses to protect himself, particularly from his colleagues. In my day you were considered some sort of an invert if you didn't carry an anti-personnel device. And you were probably killed as a result. Rightly or wrongly, I'm not going to chop logic with you on that. Because whether or not you were inverted, this was very much part of our lives.

We were schoolboys, you see. We were alert to our past. Our traditions. Our history. Look carefully into the shadows and you would see, mixing with the mist and chimney smoke, the ghosts of our medieval forebears moving in and out of the cloisters. In the faces of the Upper Fifth you might discern a Tudor lilt to the line of this cheekbone, a Norman turn to that mouth. And look there, a positively Georgian fatboy over his tuckbox eating fruitcake with both hands. You think I'm joking? Everywhere you look you see heliographs winking messages at you out of the past.

Look here in the Usher's Dayroom. Framed among the sporting portraits, a letter from Deacon Flyte, our Master in 1825. The letter begs parents to stop their boys coming back to school *with loaded firearms*. An escaping Colleger, caught by a fleet organ tutor, had fired a primitive derringer into the musicologist's skull. Frightened him to death! The organ tutor!

So let's just get back to basics for a minute. Let's just get our head out of the clouds and our feet firmly on the ground. It wasn't just advisable to carry arms in those days, it was practically compulsory. And if you were found in possession of a firearm by some master sneaking through your locker, you were, of course, immediately expelled. But expelled with honour, and you took up your

Exhibition at Magdalen with a devil-may-care expression on your face.

I like that.

You talk about violence in schools today. I don't know what you think went on in English public schools in happier times than these.

You see the Hop Quad dolly? That straw guy bent over the block with its night shirt over its head? And how passing masters swipe at the exposed backward parts with long ferrules?

In the late Middle Ages, a dispute over the boys' small beer ration escalated to the point where two clerical masters were escorted into Hop Quad by a party of senior boys and were there hanged by the neck. A bold stroke, it caught the imagination of the school. 'Hovoc! Havac!' they cried, 'Smyte hard, and give gode knockes!' as they swept out of College in a horde. They charged the village (only out of habit, the village had done nothing), staves a-hand, and knocked it senseless. The king sent in troops to calm the situation, and the boys marched victoriously back to College to cut the clerics down. By a small intervention of God, both men found they were alive. And so grateful were they that they birched the boys responsible for six or seven days before sending them off to take up their Exhibitions at Magdalen. And ever after, on the anniversary of that day . . .

What about that!

I sound as though I admire it? My dear old turkey, we couldn't do without it! Sportsmen, you see, reckless spirits, scornful of punishment. *Ave atque vale*, where are they now? I blame demand feeding.

Now then, how do you get to Salisbury College?

I suppose I must have taken Common Entrance. How

many buns in a baker's dozen and all that sort of thing. Willy, Willy, Harry, Stee. I could never see the point of examinations because it's all about the interview, isn't it? The key question is the one that starts, 'Why do you think you've been sent here?'

'Why, to scout and scamper, and fend for myself for a few years, to learn my place in the world, and fill the unforgiving minute with sixty seconds worth of distance run,' was my answer, and they gave me an Exhibition.

A couple of short years later a tug was asked the same question. He said, 'I think it's so that when my parents die I'll be used to it,' and they gave him a Scholarship. Of course a different wind had started to blow. He kept his Scholarship and they took away my Exhibition for my long division.

He was a sensitive boy. They all went like that. Shrinking souls. Would have been better for all of us if the whole generation had stayed at home with their private tutors, and Captain Pugwash every Sunday afternoon on the nursery sofa.

I've nothing against sensitive boys, don't get me wrong. I'm sensitive myself. Prick me and do I not howl with the rest of them? As a matter of fact I don't, but the point holds.

It was a different wind all right, blowing through my time at school. When I arrived at Salisbury you couldn't tell the prefects from the masters. When I took up my Exhibition at Magdalen four years later you couldn't tell the undergraduates from the servants. That's how much England had changed in four short years.

Come on, come on. Let's get on with it

Our story starts on the first day of an academic year, don't ask me which. I'd swung my old trunk off the Bentley, and seen off the parents with a cheerful wave. By God it was good to be back at school, in that crowd of old friends and new faces. Black jackets, flashing white shirts, groups in doorways reminiscing in excited terms about their summer holidays and the merits of the coming half. The peculiar scent of a Michaelmas term – woodsmoke, coaldust, fallen leaves, toasting teacakes – was in the air. The rugger posts were up. Autumn trees stood like tall fires across the country.

Look at the boy I was then, jostling through Mob Quad. Look at the shoulders on him, the strength in his step. It was the start of a great adventure that you've probably forgotten. You're fat now, and disappointed. You're taken up with your wives, and restaurants, and all the other swinish pleasures of the grown-up. But can you yet imagine what it was to be up for the XXX, and a Quarter Captain in the Half Quad game? I had a reserved place in the first fifteen for extra seconds at Low Tea – I was almost certain to get an extra doughnut on Thursdays. Don't take a lofty tone with me because you're a marketing manager now. Salisbury had been good to me.

The House Scully – ancient, oak-hearted – was carrying my trunk up Skip Staircase ('No, no, young sir, I'll manage it handily') when a laundry basket came hurtling down the staircase towards us. Wimpering was heard from it, as of a terrified new boy clinging by his little fingertips to the interior wickerwork. From the top of the stairs the cheering of the Second Year Pit and additional squealing as another tug was packed up for despatch. This really wouldn't do. I determined to put a stop to it there and then.

'Stop that bloody awful noise!' I yelled with all my authority, and it seemed to work. As the skip careered past the wimpering distinctly stopped for a moment. 'Weak-chested young puppies they are this year, sir,' Scully growled.

'Never fear Scully, we'll knock them into shape. Look out, here comes another one.'

The second skip bounced into the bannisters and lodged there, jammed. I leaned down to heave it on its way, the lid leapt up and caught me a smart blow on the bridge of the nose. Through a blur of involuntary tears I first saw him. Pale face. Flashing eyes. A lanoline gloss in his hair. Like an Afghan girl by firelight.

'Is it very much further to go?' he piped unhappily. I stood there holding my face in silence. It must have been the blow to my nose for I was incapable of thought. Any thought.

Scully swung the lid shut and rolled him away into the darkness. 'Cheeky little beggar,' Scully growled and of course he was absolutely right. That boy in the skip, with the eyes of an Afghan girl, was to become the most famous and most destructive little tart in Salisbury's history. I don't blame him. I blame myself. Though pity knows, it wasn't my fault.

Now listen. If I say I sensed it then, with the tears starting as I watched him tumbling down the darkness. If I say what I sensed then with his face still glowing in the dark. If I say that Time turned on itself. If I say what I saw in that deformity. That I saw passages, and conduits, and oubliettes of history. That I saw a secret room, and a fair boy sitting in someone's lap and ruffling his hair . . . what would you think of me then? I'll tell you. You'd think me an unreliable witness. I am keen that you believe me through what follows so I merely say that I shrugged off a sense of large unease, and mounted the steps to the Long Chamber.

Come too, oh yes, you have to come as well. You'll have a large sense of unease too, if you've got any sense. Scully heaves my trunk alongside, and the sound of our footsteps bounces around the stone walls. You'd like to hold my hand now, I dare say, but I *fear* I am a little preoccupied at the moment. No, no, there are larger things on my mind. You better hold your own hand – but don't let anybody see.

There is a door ahead, with iron studs, and an old handle. Turn the handle, lean on the door, you will see something you will never forget.

Look into the Long Chamber

There is a roar of young voices as the door opens, and you've a moment to look about your new home. It's not a pretty sight.

It is a vast, dark dormitory. It is vaulted above and dark below. Windows are set higher than you'd think in the bare walls. These are spartan quarters; you will find them harsh till they have hardened you to them. But take a deep breath. There is at least firelight. In the dancing shadows, on a raised chair beside the Black Prince's Block sits the Head of our House with a devotional text. A College Blood sits with his boots on the fender of the fire. He reads a racing paper as he smokes his pipe. A small boy brushes the Blood's hair as they evaluate the betting together. A nude walks down the boards to the bathroom, a towel slung over his shoulder. Two practise with quarterstaves – clack! clack! clack! 'A quatre I think!' 'Damn you, my head!' There is scrumming round a tuckbox, and a sudden drive over the beds as one breaks away with a fruitcake.

A poker school is in progress. On a crossbeam, high above the beds, above the glow of candles and hanging lamps, a small group sits with its Bibles. The Shell throw conkers at it, and frequently hit it. You can't see why these are called your happiest days, but you will.

Down the dark end, where there is little light and no fire, that is where the new tugs go to huddle. They are indistinct. They are not really there at all. They are half at home with their sisters, with their family dog, half tucked up in their truckle beds with a teddy bear in their bottom drawer. They are only half here in Salisbury, in the Long Chamber, by themselves.

It all presents a vivid and mysterious scene. An eventful night beneath the hammerbeams will tell you everything you need to know about a man. Masters have no authority here. They have no standing in the Long Chamber. This is shown in the exchange between the Master and your mother.

'Master, may we see where the boys eat, and sleep?'

'Madam, I have never seen where the boys "eat" and "sleep" myself. They appear in morning school rested. They seem to have been fed. We must assume the appointments are satisfactory. Some things are better left to faith and hope than to charity.'

This was the world of the old public schools. We were boys together. We were all of us boys in the Long Chamber. There was none of the civilising effect of women. The Housemaster was unmarried, and the matron played hockey for Lancashire. As boys we fell into our places, and there was a place for everyone. A smaller place for the inconspicuous, but a place nonetheless.

Here – stand shoulder-to-shoulder with your contemporaries and look about you. It's no wonder you're on edge. You're to be taken on your merits (you won't like that). You are small and shy; you are 13 years old. Faces break in and out of the shadows like carnival masks. The questions that loom large in your young mind are these:

1) Who are all these people?
2) What are they going to do to you?

You have been delivered to a door by a Scully who has

only knuckled his head and said nothing. He has shown you in and craftily shut the door behind. You wait with your trunk. To answer the question when it is shouted along a pointed finger: 'You sir! What's your name!'

I can do nothing for you. I'm looking for my friend Cavendish. We're in the same cell this half. He's a particular friend of mine. He has twenty juniors you know – you'll find out about that. He's a sportsman, and clever with it. And you should see the way he dresses!

'Cavendish! My dear fellow!'

'Wynn-Candy! How are you, old horse!'

'All the better for seeing you!'

'Who are these little sprigs?'

'These? Haven't a clue! Off you go now. Cut along, you live down there somewhere. You'll find your name on the bed. Cavendish, I must tell you the funniest thing.'

'What's that, Wynn-Candy?'

'We got a pig drunk and let him loose in the bazaar!'

'A pig! Don't tell me!'

As you move away from this tantalising conversation you hope to pass unnoticed. Which all of you do . . . except one. Carnahan, in the fancy waistcoat, looks up at you with a terrible expression and cries, 'You sir! What's your name!' And you say, 'Me? My name's Robertshaw.' And that is your first mistake.

Robertshaw? The Head of House looks up from his text. Robertshaw? The Blood drops his pipe. What sort of Robertshaw? The quarterstaves fall silent. The poker school lays down its cards. The beam boys swing nimbly to the floor. And Carnahan picks up that cane. What is he going to do with that cane?

'Well, say quickly: are you a Hog Robertshaw or a Peely-Po Robertshaw?'

We all whooped at the expression on his face. It's not the easiest question in the world to answer, if you've never been asked it before.

'I really couldn't say,' he said. 'I'm one of the Robertshaws from Mildmay Road in Islington, if that's any use to you?'

'*Use* to us? Use to *us*?' Carnahan roared in his comic way. 'Answer at once. Are you a Hog Robertshaw? No? Then you must be a Peely-Po! You must be! That's the way it works!'

'Are you Hog or Peely-Po! Is he Hog or Peely-Po?' Cavendish offered me a cocked arm to jig upon and we gaily spun to the accompaniment of an impromptu reed instrument.

'Is he Hog or Peely-po?
That is what we have to know.
Yes to Hog is no to Po,
This is how the dance must go.
Before that boy takes off his shoes
We really must insist he choose!'

He looked at us sideways, closed his eyes and waited. We admired pluck in our House. But we didn't like cheek. No, we *hated* cheek. Then he put his thumb in his trousers, in a way we had seen in American films (he really was making a very poor start), and said: 'I have come back from the Cape (that's in South Africa). There you cannot choose the side you are on. Now that I have a choice, I choose not to be on any side at all.'

I seem to remember he was hung from a beam for this. Not immediately (we were in Governor's Grace). And there will be the question of the potato, so we better get the subject of bullying out of the way at once.

On bullying

Of course there was never any bullying.

The tugs were not treated by aunts, we were not aunties to our tugs, but bullying? I won't have that said. No sir! I will not! Then off with your spectacles and up with your fists, we'll settle this matter out of court.

I don't care if you *are* the Chairman of British Oxygen, get those glasses off!

Of course it's not pleasant the first night at your public school. It's bewildering and it hurts. It's a night exercise in crocodile country. You've no idea what's going on. Bells ring; you don't know what they mean but everyone starts moving. Corridors go off into the warren, and you don't know where they lead. Your collar doesn't fit and the stud hurts. You stand outside doors and daren't knock to know who's in there. Then a grown man throws you out of a window. You long – oh how you long – for the nursery sofa, with a pint of cocoa, and your sister, and Captain Pugwash on the television.

Of course you do, you've never been so alone in your life, and we assume you're only human. That's why we had to attract their attention at once, that first night. Otherwise – the poor little beasts – they descend into introspection, and no man's character can stand too much introspection.

No, nor no boy's either.

These boys, let us say, these brothers, these *Robertshaws*, in some century or other, they disagreed about the way you should eat potato. The one preferred potato in its skin (Hog Robertshaw). The other liked it peeled (Peely-Po Robertshaw). They couldn't agree, and so they went to Scratch for an eighty-seven-round bare-knuckle fight after which one of them died, probably. Ever after, any Robertshaw in College had to declare himself for one or the other. That at least speaks for itself. And it reflected well on us in College. 'We've got a Robertshaw in our House, you know.' 'Really? Hog or Peely-Po?' 'Peely-Po, but none the worse for that.' 'Good man!'

Perfectly simple, perfectly straightforward. Perhaps you think we hadn't explained it carefully enough before hanging him from the beam? Well, strictly speaking we hadn't explained it at all, he was supposed to take it on faith.

'But it doesn't make any sense!' you want to say.

Well of course it doesn't make any sense. But what, you

need everything to make sense? In this day and age? What sense is there in those two benders in three-button Burton suits walking off with the £10,000 Turner prize? And here's a state beneficiary who's poured liquid wart remover into his baby's eyes – any ideas on that one? And England hasn't won a rugger match since Suez, and you talk about wanting things to make sense.

Let us be realistic.

Consider. How else were we to draw a tug out of the kennel of his prep-school self and introduce him to the mysteries of life in a public school? You can't do that and make sense. You can't *do* both.

So picture a roomful of new tugs. They are sitting in fretful conversation groups at the black table. They are tiny in their vast collars and sleeves over their knuckles, and tailcoats down past their knees. Your heart would open up to them if you let it. You'd have their mothers in, and a little television, and set aside a quiet half-hour for them to watch Captain Pugwash. But they wouldn't thank you for it in the end. They are poor creatures. They are not men, not boys. Just up from their kids' schools. Captain of their kids' XVs. Matrons' favourites and famous for their raffia work. But not Salisbury men. Not by a mile. Not yet. The change would take an alchemy, and we were the alchemists.

So what were the sort of things we did to them? Oh, I can hardly remember now. Me, I never liked to do it, particularly, I did it out of duty. But I didn't dislike it either, there's nothing funny about me.

The tugs lived in a room a dozen steps down from the Long Chamber. It was called The Pit. I spent a year there myself. Fine room. Awful place. I liked it less than Kettners. But then you weren't *supposed* to like The Pit, that was the point of the place.

A low, dark, Norman room it was. Lot of black oak in it. Tall lockers fitted to the walls by Richard II. A ceiling porcupine-full of dip-quill pens. Along one wall, a gallery gave out onto the room, and from this we can observe the tugs at work and play. They can't see us for the lights in their eyes. But they know something is up: they are dressed in a strange and impressive way. One is a Foundation Scholar and wears a gown. Nonetheless, when a Second Year man shouts 'Tug!' even Foundation Scholars must obey.

A man in the gallery shouted 'Tug!' and all the tugs who were sitting down stood up, and all the tugs standing up sat down. If he says 'Tug! Tug! Tug!', they do it three times. If he says it ten times, they do it ten times. They did it as long and as often as required. Boring? Oh my aunt, you can have no idea how boring it was, but there it was, we had to do it:

Tug! (up) Tug! (down) Tug! (up) Tug! (down) Tug! (up) Tug! (down)
Tug! (up) Tug! (down) Tug! (up) Tug! (down) Tug! (up) Tug! (down)
Tug! (up) Tug! (down) Tug! (up) Tug! (down) Tug! (up) Tug! (down)
Tug! (up) Tug! (down) Tug! (up) Tug! (down) Tug! (up) Tug! (down)
Tug! (up) Tug! (down) Tug! (up) Tug! (down) Tug! (up) Tug! (down)
Tug! (up) Tug! (down) Tug! (up) Tug! (down) Tug! (up) Tug! (down)
Tug! (up) Tug! (down) Tug! (up) Tug! (down) Tug! (up) Tug! (down)
Tug! (up) Tug! (down) Tug! (up) Tug! (down) Tug! (up) Tug! (down)
Tug! (up) Tug! (down) Tug! (up) Tug! (down) Tug! (up) Tug! (down)
Tug! (up) Tug! (down) Tug! (up) Tug! (down) Tug! (up) Tug! (down)
Tug! (up) Tug! (down) Tug! (up) Tug! (down) Tug! (up) Tug! (down)
Tug! (up) Tug! (down) Tug! (up) Tug! (down) Tug! (up) Tug! (down)
Tug! (up) Tug! (down) Tug! (up) Tug! (down) Tug! (up) Tug! (down)
Tug! (up) Tug! (down) Tug! (up) Tug! (down) Tug! (up) Tug! (down)
Tug! (up) Tug! (down) Tug! (up) Tug! (down) Tug! (up) Tug! (down)
Tug! (up) Tug! (down) Tug! (up) Tug! (down) Tug! (up) Tug! (down)
Tug! (up) Tug! (down) Tug! (up) Tug! (down) Tug! (up) Tug! (down)
Tug! (up) Tug! (down) Tug! (up) Tug! (down) Tug! (up) Tug! (down)
Tug! (up) Tug! (down) Tug! (up) Tug! (down) Tug! (up) Tug! (down)
Tug! (up) Tug! (down) Tug! (up) Tug! (down) Tug! (up) Tug! (down)
Tug! (up) Tug! (down) Tug! (up) Tug! (down) Tug! (up) Tug! (down)
Tug! (up) Tug! (down) Tug! (up) Tug! (down) Tug! (up) Tug! (down)
Tug! (up) Tug! (down) Tug! (up) Tug! (down) Tug! (up) Tug! (down)
Tug! (up) Tug! (down) Tug! (up) Tug! (down) Tug! (up) Tug! (down)
Tug! (up) Tug! (down) Tug! (up) Tug! (down) Tug! (up) Tug! (down)
Tug! (up) Tug! (down) Tug! (up) Tug! (down) Tug! (up) Tug! (down)
Tug! (up) Tug! (down) Tug! (up) Tug! (down) Tug! (up) Tug! (down)
Tug! (up) Tug! (down) Tug! (up) Tug! (down) Tug! (up) Tug! (down)

Tug! (up) Tug! (down) Tug! (up) Tug! (down) Tug! (up) Tug! (down)
Tug! (up) Tug! (down) Tug! (up) Tug! (down) Tug! (up) Tug! (down)

Had enough yet? It goes on forever, doesn't it? You start to dream about it at night. Awfully boring, even in a dream.

Tug! (down) Tug! (up) Tug! (down) Tug! (up) Tug! (down) Tug! (up)
Tug! (down) Tug! (up) Tug! (down) Tug! (up) Tug! (down) Tug! (up)
Tug! (down) Tug! (up) Tug! (down) Tug! (up) Tug! (down) Tug! (up)
Tug! (down) Tug! (up) Tug! (down) Tug! (up) Tug! (down) Tug! (up)
Tug! (down) Tug! (up) Tug! (down) Tug! (up) Tug! (down) Tug! (up)
Tug! (down) Tug! (up) Tug! (down) Tug! (up) Tug! (down) Tug! (up)
Tug! (down) Tug! (up) Tug! (down) Tug! (up) Tug! (down) Tug! (up)
Tug! (down) Tug! (up) Tug! (down) Tug! (up) Tug! (down) Tug! (up)
Tug! (down) Tug! (up) Tug! (down) Tug! (up) Tug! (down) Tug! (up)
Tug! (down) Tug! (up) Tug! (down) Tug! (up) Tug! (down) Tug! (up)
Tug! (down) Tug! (up) Tug! (down) Tug! (up) Tug! (down) Tug! (up)
Tug! (down) Tug! (up) Tug! (down) Tug! (up) Tug! (down) Tug! (up)
Tug! (down) Tug! (up) Tug! (down) Tug! (up) Tug! (down) Tug! (up)
Tug! (down) Tug! (up) Tug! (down) Tug! (up) Tug! (down) Tug! (up)
Tug! (down) Tug! (up) Tug! (down) Tug! (up) Tug! (down) Tug! (up)
Tug! (down) Tug! (up) Tug! (down) Tug! (up) Tug! (down) Tug! (up)
Tug! (down) Tug! (up) Tug! (down) Tug! (up) Tug! (down) Tug! (up)
Tug! (down) Tug! (up) Tug! (down) Tug! (up) Tug! (down) Tug! (up)
Tug! (down) Tug! (up) Tug! (down) Tug! (up) Tug! (down) Tug! (up)
Tug! (down) Tug! (up) Tug! (down) Tug! (up) Tug! (down) Tug! (up)
Tug! (down) Tug! (up) Tug! (down) Tug! (up) Tug! (down) Tug! (up)
Tug! (down) Tug! (up) Tug! (down) Tug! (up) Tug! (down) Tug! (up)
Tug! (down) Tug! (up) Tug! (down) Tug! (up) Tug! (down) Tug! (up)
Tug! (down) Tug! (up) Tug! (down) Tug! (up) Tug! (down) Tug! (up)
Tug! (down) Tug! (up) Tug! (down) Tug! (up) Tug! (down) Tug! (up)
Tug! (down) Tug! (up) Tug! (down) Tug! (up) Tug! (down) Tug! (up)
Tug! (down) Tug! (up) Tug! (down) Tug! (up) Tug! (down) Tug! (up)
Tug! (down) Tug! (up) Tug! (down) Tug! (up) Tug! (down) Tug! (up)
Tug! (down) Tug! (up) Tug! (down) Tug! (up) Tug! (down) Tug! (up)
Tug! (down) Tug! (up) Tug! (down) Tug! (up) Tug! (down) Tug! (up)
Tug! (down) Tug! (up) Tug! (down) Tug! (up) Tug! (down) Tug! (up)
Tug! (down) Tug! (up) Tug! (down) Tug! (up) Tug! (down) Tug! (up)
Tug! (down) Tug! (up) Tug! (down) Tug! (up) Tug! (down) Tug! (up)

Oh my hat, you've finished your banana and you're not halfway through. The things you do at school because you have to.

Tug! (up) Tug! (down) Tug! (up) Tug! (down) Tug! (up) Tug! (down) Tug!
(up) Tug! (down) Tug! (up) Tug! (down) Tug! (up) Tug! (down) Tug! (up)
Tug! (down) Tug! (up) Tug! (down) Tug! (up) Tug! (down) Tug! (up) Tug!
(down) Tug! (up) Tug! (down) Tug! (up) Tug! (down) Tug! (up) Tug!
(down) Tug! (up) Tug! (down) Tug! (up) Tug! (down) Tug! (up) Tug!
(down) Tug! (up) Tug! (down) Tug! (up) Tug! (down) Tug! (up) Tug!
(down) Tug! (up) Tug! (down) Tug! (up) Tug! (down) Tug! (up) Tug!
(down) Tug! (up) Tug! (down) Tug! (up) Tug! (down) Tug! (up) Tug!
(down) Tug! (up) Tug!
(down) Tug! (up) Tug!
(down) Tug! (up) Tug!
(down) Tug! (up) Tug!
(down) Tug! (up) Tug!
(down) Tug! (up) Tug!
(down) Tug! (up) Tug!
(down) Tug! (up) Tug!
(down) Tug! (up) Tug!
(down) Tug! (up) Tug!
(down) Tug! (up) Tug!
(down) Tug! (up) Tug!
(down) Tug! (up) Tug!
(down) Tug! (up) Tug!
(down) Tug! (up) Tug!
(down) Tug! (up) Tug!
(down) Tug! (up) Tug!
(down) Tug! (up) Tug!
(down) Tug! (up) Tug!
(down) Tug! (up) Tug!
(down) Tug! (up) Tug!
(down) Tug! (up) Tug!
(down) Tug! (up) Tug!
(down) Tug! (up) Tug!
(down) Tug! (up) Tug!
(down) Tug! (up) Tug!
(down) Tug! (up) Tug!
(down) Tug! (up) Tug!
(down) Tug! (up) Tug!
(down) Tug! (up) Tug!
(down) Tug! (up) Tug!
(down) Tug! (up) Tug!
(down) Tug! (up) Tug!

Tug! Tug! Tug! (up) Tug!Tug!Tug! down
Tug! Tug! Tug! (up) Tug!Tug!Tug! down
Tug! Tug! Tug! (up) Tug!Tug!Tug! down
Tug! Tug! Tug! (up) Tug!Tug!Tug! down
Tug! (up) Tug! (down)
Tug! (up) Tug! (down)
Tug! (up) Tug! (down)
Tug! (up) Tug! (down)
Tug! (up) Tug! (down)
Tug! (up) Tug! (down)
Tug! (up) Tug! (down)
Tug! (up) Tug! (down)
Tug! (up) Tug! (down)
Tug! (up) Tug! (down)
Tug! (up) Tug! (down)
Tug! (up) Tug! (down)
Tug! (up) Tug! (down)
Tug! (up) Tug! (down)
Tug! (up) Tug! (down)
Tug! (up) Tug! (down)
Tug! (up) Tug! (down)
Tug! (up) Tug! (down)
Tug! (up) Tug! (down)
Tug! (up) Tug! (down)
Tug! (up) Tug! (down)
Tug! (up) Tug! (down)
Tug! (up) Tug! (down)
Tug! (up) Tug! (down)
Tug! (up) Tug! (down)
Tug! (up) Tug! (down)
Tug! (up) Tug! (down)
Tug! (up) Tug! (down)
Tug! (up) Tug! (down)
Tug! (up) Tug! (down)
Tug! (up) Tug! (down)
Tug! (up) Tug! (down)
Tug! (up) Tug! (down)
Tug! (up) Tug! (down)
Tug! (up) Tug! (down)
Tug! (up) Tug! (down)
Tug! (up) Tug! (down)
Tug! (up)Tug! (down)
(down)

Tug! (up) Tug! (down) Tug! (up) Tug! (down)
Tug! (up) Tug! (down) Tug! (up) Tug! (down)
Tug! (up) Tug! (down) Tug! (up) Tug! (down) Tug!
(up) Tug! (down) Tug! (up) Tug! (down) Tug! (up) Tug!
(down) Tug! (up) Tug! (down) Tug! (up) Tug! (down) Tug! (up)   Tug!
(down) Tug!   (up) Tug! (down)
Tug! (up) Tug!   (down) Tug! (up)
Tug! (down) Tug!   (up) Tug! (down)
Tug! (up) Tug!   (down) Tug! (up)
Tug! (down) Tug!
Tug! (up) Tug!
Tug! (down) Tug!
Tug! (up) Tug!
Tug! (down) Tug!
Tug! (up) Tug!
Tug! (down) Tug!
Tug! (up) Tug!
Tug! (down) Tug!
Tug! (up) Tug!
Tug! (down) Tug!
Tug! (up) Tug!
Tug! (down) Tug!
Tug! (up) Tug!
Tug! (down) Tug!
Tug! (up) Tug!
Tug! (down) Tug!
Tug! (up) Tug!   Tug! (down) Tug! (up) Tug! (down)
Tug! (down) Tug!   Tug! (down) Tug! (up) Tug! (down)
Tug! (up) Tug!   Tug! (down) Tug! (up) Tug! (down)
Tug! (down) Tug!   Tug! (up) Tug! (down)
Tug! (up) Tug!   Tug! (up) Tug! (down)
Tug! (down) Tug!   Tug! (up) Tug! (down)
Tug! (up) Tug!   Tug! (down) Tug! (up)
Tug! (down) Tug!   Tug! (up) Tug!
Tug! (up) Tug!   Tug! (down) Tug!
Tug! (up) Tug! (down) Tug! (up) Tug! (down)
Tug! (up) Tug! (down) Tug! (up) Tug! (down)
Tug! (up) Tug! (down) Tug! (up) Tug!
(down) Tug! (up) Tug! (down)
Tug! (up) Tug!

You'd be weeping with boredom if you had to go through this more than twice a day. It was not pleasant *but someone had to do it.* And do it we did, watching with approval as our tugs went up and down like a sixteen-valve piston engine.

Skillful tugs were able to continue their studies while moving like this, and eat a banana at the same time. So before you get on your high horse, remember it wasn't such an imposition on their time as Tug Pick-up (half a pound of scattered confetti), or on their clothes as Tug Scrum (a forty-minute maul in the middle of the room), or on their stomachs as Tug Soup (a five-pint boil-up of bootwax and vinegar mopped up with wadding polish).

Meaningless, you say? Degrading?

Ah, but you wear your hair in a ponytail, don't you. Just remember this: a trained dog has the freedom of the field. An untrained dog can never be let off the leash. *So which is the happier hound?*

But boys, you say – you want to drive me into a corner – are not to be compared with dogs?

Well that shows how much you know about dogs. Ask any mother. I think you've just defeated your own argument.

There was no bullying in Salisbury College.

But every school memoir that's ever been written . . .

Yes, yes, yes.

All right, all right.

ALL RIGHT! I said.

There were exceptions. My fagmaster was a fair man, for instance, but he was exceptionally cruel. Fair but cruel. When they barely prevented him from plugging a tug into a system of electrical socketry of his own design he left College on the next train. He now runs an interrogation service for a group of American fruit companies in Latin America. But he was the exception that proves the rule.

The regime was humane. We protected the weak. And if it was themselves we had to protect them from, so be it. It was not a pleasant job, but someone had to do it. That was the kind of men we were in those days. We wouldn't duck our duty. It would have been easy to turn our backs on them – God knows we had more enjoyable things to do with our time.

Though don't think it was a sort of saintliness that made us kick the tugs into shape. We needed them for reasons of our own. For our future generations of classes, choirs, cadres, chorus lines, and reinforcements when the town yobs came at us with knobkerries. It was enlightened self-interest of the most practical kind.

No, but primitive, you say. You agree with the reasoning (who couldn't?) But *you just don't like the sound of it.* It rings in your ear with a harsh note. You think it's primitive, barbaric, tribalistic.

Well *clearly* it was barbarous, primitive, tribalistic. But before you get carried away with comfortable indignation in your armchair there, I must assure you that we never planted large denomination coinage in the foreskins of our tugs as the Inkudulu do. We never carved cabbalistic mandalas on their chins in the way of the Choykuyu. We did not sit them on anthills as the Barandabili do, and sing comic songs in their faces. So don't invest too much critical energy in the tribal line of thinking: in comparison we were aunties! We were aunties to our tugs compared with them.

And with the admiration afforded these days to primitive, barbarous, tribal communities I'm amazed British public schools weren't afforded more respect.

So be serious for a minute. It was a false kindness to go easy on the tugs. They had a lot to learn. A body of knowledge equivalent to a foreign language O-Level in two weeks.

Knowledge was vital to the young tug. 'He that increaseth knowledge increaseth sorrow,' it says in Ecclesiastes, and we have to take it in good faith. But without knowledge of the normal business practice of Salisbury College, you would be in a more desperately sorry state still.

This is boring, but you have to know it

There is a lot to learn about life in Salisbury College. I'm going to canter you through a day. Give you an idea of the routine. I'm also going to teach you how to shirk, so pay attention. We'll start at first light.

6.30: Bells for ice-breaking (here's something Salisbury taught me: no hangover can survive really cold water). The tugs have to be in their slippers, bent over a basin by the time the bells stop ringing. There were duties for the tugs after that – iron the newspapers, that sort of thing. Bring the Usher his basin of warm water. It was boiled up over the open fire. We'd had hot running water for a hundred years, but boys are creatures of habit.

Then an hour in your various quarters (Pit, Cell, Study, Room) to finish yesterday's prep (*Caesar adsum jam forte*: classics. Latin, actually). Often an hour spent playing dot cricket for a world team headed by Henry V, and working up your grip on a tennis ball.

7.45: scrum down for breakfast (and what a scrum it was). Twelve gallons of milk, one hundred loaves, butter and bits and pieces were left in the buttery hatches by the Scullies' wives who left the hall in very short order ('Molly, for the love of God, you can't go back for your dropped ribbon, are you mad!') Breakfast was distributed amongst College boys strictly according to the strength of their personalities. Owing to this early training, many of us went on to do well on the floor of the Stock Exchange.

8.15: back to House. Supervise the Bedders, quiz the tugs

on the day's menu. A keen young tug could recite the menu for three meals in eight seconds. He couldn't understand a blind thing he was saying at that speed, and neither could you, but it created a sense of common purpose.

8.30: Morning Service in Chapel. This isn't as easy as it seems, you better listen carefully to this. I better dwell a bit on this one, for this is the way we walk to worship. It's 250 yards through complicated ground, so sit up at the back there.

To walk to Matins we must leave the relative safety of the Long Chamber and descend the spiral staircase. We're all right so far, they won't flack us here while we've got reinforcements at hand. But there's a corridor going off to three other Houses, and we have sacked more Houses this year than have sacked us: they might get together against us. Especially down here on the ground floor as we break out into Dean's Yard.

Now, the first thing you must realise is that we are technically out of bounds. And yet it is the only way we have into College. There is no other way. If you confront a master –and they pass this way as often as we do – you are liable to be flogged for breaking bounds. You wouldn't like to be flogged. Wouldn't care for the pain of it. *But*, there has never been a flogging for this offence.

What is the reason for this strange paradox? It is because masters and boys collaborate in the practice of shirking. Let me teach you how to shirk. You'll be quizzed on this for your Liberties, so get it right. In the area now known as Dean's Yard, there was, at the time of the Wars of the Roses, a chop house which lay outside the school's boundary. The chop house keeper had a lovely daughter. By night the boys were up and down the ivy to her room with their flintlock lanthorns. And the shadows they made together on the walls preyed so on the chop house keeper's mind that he burnt them all: potboys, scholars, daughter, and all his chops. He smiled as he warmed himself in front of the fire, before the Nightwatch came to take him away.

Why were the boys up and down the ivy? Oh, I've really no idea.

The college bought the ashes and land and built the Long Chamber. The important thing was: they didn't change the statutes allowing legal access to the Long Chamber. The land was as much out of bounds as it had ever been, no matter that we now owned the land. But don't go thinking that tradition suffocated us. The boys of the Long Chamber clearly had to communicate with College. The practicalities of life would not be ignored in favour of blind obedience.

So shirking came to pass. A master will pretend not to see you as long as you make a decent attempt not to be seen. So if a master is heading your way and there is a doorway, you step into it. If there isn't a doorway, you turn and walk in the other direction. Obviously you don't overtake a master walking in front of you. The larger, slower masters could thus jam a back-up of fifty or sixty boys over the length of Welsh Walk. If time is running short, the master will find himself the object of comment ('Trot on!', or 'Trot on, you ruminant!' or 'Trot on, you indolent hippo!') and only the most insensitive man could maintain his measured tread. Only the most hardened might turn and actually face his following. Here, the sub-clauses of shirking demand all boys to turn their faces to the wall and cover them with book or hand. If the master has accurately calculated his prestige he will see a thicket of books and hands. If he has misjudged his status he will be trampled.

All in all, a thoroughly intelligent and practical solution to the problem. It allowed change without changing anything. And that takes talent.

So let's see if you've got the hang of it. Here we are in Dean's Yard coming up behind the organ tutor. What do we do?

No, no, no!

We *don't* hang behind. We sweep contemptuously past him (an organ tutor lacks the seniority to be shirked, he is not shirkable). But *get back*, *get back*, get into that doorway, we studiously shirk with a thrill of submission one of the Praeposters – who is still called a boy though he is over twenty years of age, has two children and a moustache. He has stayed on at school for a couple of years, trying annually for his Exhibition to Magdalen.

9.00: now what? After Chapel there were lessons, I assume. *Pompei aderat. Caesar sic in omnibus. Pompei in is at.* Or was that prep school? I think that was prep school. You're assuming I was thick? Well what are the principal parts of *subfero* then? You think you know but you don't.

11.00: morning go-down. We have a half-hour for doughnuts. If it's a second Thursday in the month the Half Quad game is played. A toiling mass of collarless boys in Half Quad strive to score a goal. The study windows throng with young faces, waste paper baskets are clattered with rulers, and occasionally the metal baskets are thrown down into the mêlée. The game didn't have a ball, it used a small boy called a Goat. The poet Alexander Pope played a crucial role in the last goal ever scored (he was thrown through a first floor window in 1690).

12.45: lunch. Quite a different atmosphere from breakfast. You weren't allowed to ask for things. You had to say 'I doubt I would actually die of disgust if I had some gravy,' and they'd pass you the gravy. Bad manners (wrong fork, spraying food, starting a fist fight) were punished: you had to make up an epigram, and if you didn't have an epigram in you, you paid a Foundation Scholar in the Trading Quarter to do it for you.

1.30: games. Hooray. We'll come to games.

5.00: afternoon school. We've been through that.

6.45: dinner. Beef and small beer.

7.15: prep. Henry V scores a thousand runs, Adolf Hitler caught on the boundary. You can only play dot cricket alone in your cell because the other fellows laugh at you if they catch you at it. I should have given it up years ago, I was aware of that perfectly well. It just happens that I've never particularly grown out of it. I used to play it in Aden while the SAS were throwing people out of helicopters. And I still believe I was better employed than they.

9.00: absence. A call for the whole house. '*Adsum, adsum, adsum* . . .' Announcements made. Public congratulations for top work. Others were beaten.

10.00: lights out

6.30: Bells.

So now you know. Not that you do, of course. You hardly know the first thing yet, I'm warning you.

Talk, talk talk! For God's sake let's get out on the pitch!

The ball soars up off a boot into a cobalt sky. The autumn air scythes into your lungs as you rip across the pitch. Falling leaves fill the air like a flock of birds. Brilliant clouds tear across the sky. A fancy winger is running at you with his elbows akimbo and his heels kicking out too far to the side. Bang! He's scooped up at the knees, knocked off his feet, but he hands the ball up to you ('My dear fellow'). And there is the broad green pitch with the creosote lines laid out like a running track ahead. Can you remember the power you had in those days to get off the mark? How your thighs worked when you said 'go!' Socks held up by garters to an inch of their position even though it was wet? And the turf lit up in the last of the low sun. There are two sets of scrums over there in a swamp-mist of their own breath. They've run too much. And coming in fast at ten and two o'clock two centres running low at you with their arms spread sideways. The shouts of boys ('Pass!' 'Tackle!' 'Go forward!' 'To me!' 'To me!' 'To me!') fill your ears as you charge the twenty-five.

During my time at Salisbury, public opinion judged a fellow very much on the way he behaved in public: how does he cope when the Warden speaks to him? How does he hold himself when the Bloods bear down on him in Mob Quad? How does he contain himself when the Sultan of Molucca lands on his person for the eighth time? When a fellow is conspicuous he held himself up for judgement. This was why none of us cared to be conspicuous. But this is important: *on the football pitch, everyone was conspicuous.*

Football was taken seriously at my school, yes by every school at the time. We have been criticised for it. By idiots, but criticism by anyone is hurtful. Football is a revealing game if you've got an eye for character. The way a man runs, for instance, will tell you everything you need to know about him. That at least needs no explanation.

I want to introduce you to the running styles of three or four players, all at different stages of their careers, and all very different sorts, but they will be important to us. They are as follows. Delavera, one of the College Praesidium, and a Sixth Form Swell. Carnahan, in the Upper Fifth, too young yet for office, but groomed for it in our Roof. Cavendish, my particular friend, and two tugs.

When Delavera ran he seemed to lift off the surface of the pitch in an effortless manner, like a sloop with the breeze in its sails. In his sidestep he accelerated through vain tackles, swinging his hair out of his eyes. In between steps he seemed to hang in the air a moment. His heels floated out behind him, gracefully, lazily. *He never hurried.* No, not when the opposition backs cut through and went for the lines. Almost lazily he was there for the tackle. No, he wouldn't hurry, but when a high ball went down the field, he'd collect it a step before the pursuers and put it into touch without their touching him. To see Delavera run for the try line made you feel like a Red Indian seeing a horse for the first time.

When Carnahan ran he inflated his chest, tucked in his chin, and clenched his fists which he punched up at his head at every other step. When checked he resented it. Then his feet would pound like an ethnic drum festival.

When making for the line he held out a straight arm in front like the punch-ram of a slave-galley (you tried not to run into it). But you wouldn't have to rely on Carnahan's running style to delineate his character. He could see it in his face which was puckered and buckled with violent emotions.

When Cavendish ran, he leant forward with his weight on the balls of his feet; he kept his hands lower than you or I would. He kept them ready to swing this way or that, to pass or to deceive the opposition in one of his elaborate feinting fits. Or to mop his rather voluptuous face with a bright red handkerchief.

Delavera lives in Brook Street, Carnahan's in the Gulf, and Cavendish was called to the Bar. You could have predicted it from watching the first training game we had that term. But then, why would you have wanted to?

Delavera said to me: 'Now then, Wynn-Candy. These tugs. Are they going to be creditable tugs, or a tapful of drips? Find out for me, will you, put them up and down the pitch half a dozen times.' He spoke to me! You've no idea how my heart swelled, to be spoken to like that by one such as Delavera. No, you don't understand. You're girls or something, you wouldn't understand.

Following our rule, then, we will watch the tugs and will learn nothing about their characters at all. Tugs, you see, don't have running styles. You'd cringe if you saw a tug with a running style. Such a thing would have the same embarrassing effect as an eight-year-old boy with a brief case. So this scene should be unilluminating. But let us see if you have an eye for it.

Our tugs are running up and down the pitch. They run upright with their forearms parallel to the turf, in that stiff way small boys have. This is their first outing so they exert themselves. There is a fat tug toiling. There is tall tug who bends in three places. There are two small tugs with round little faces. But what is this? Here are two tugs running in a conspicuous way. Two tugs have their arms held out from their shoulders. They are wheeling as they run and are simulating the sound of First World War aircraft through spluttering lips. What does this mean? Are they Dadaists?

One of them we have glimpsed. He still has not declared himself Hog or Peely-Po. The other we have also met. The little tic from the skip with the eyes of the Afghan girl. He was the one who started squealing during tackle practice and ran away from the tug he was meant to tackle, calling for the ball to be passed to him.

'Hi! You! What do you think you're playing at?'

He came up and stood too close to me. He looked at me. I didn't like it when he did that. It was my fault, I dare say, for looking back, but something odd started to happen in the back of my head as I looked at him. A sort of swirling feeling, as though a part of my brain was going down a drain. How did he do that? You saw the way the strong little eyelashes were set into his eyelids, you saw the gloss on his cheeks, and your brain started going down a drain in the back of your head.

He said, 'It is a trick, it sometimes works. You confuse the fellow into thinking you're on the same side.' He stood up very straight when he spoke, small as he was. There was a sway in his back, and an impudent look, an . . . *impudent* look in his face. The sun caught a highlight on the inside of his lower lip. Cavendish and I looked at each other with mulish expressions and we walked away.

'Someone's going to have their work cut out with that little imp,' I noted. I didn't expect it to be me.

I had taken an outside pass from Deniston and was making down the wing; their centre had travelled quickly and was coming in fast to force me into touch; his outstretched arm was too eager. I caught his hand and flung him in front of me headlong. The fullback got caught up in the sprawling legs and I jumped over the pair of them and lengthened my stride for the tryline. Then Dr de Zoete on the touchline caught me in the throat with the crook handle of his stick. He was an eccentric old bird, our Housemaster.

'I want to talk to you Wynn-Candy, come with me,' he

said. Casting a longing look at the game (a penetrating kick had gone way back down the field) I followed the old coot. 'There is a boy come under our Roof this term, and he is not as other boys. He is different from other boys. I knew his mother once, and she was not as other boys are either.'

I saw a cloud forming behind the trees, a darkness sort of gathering over the fields. Quite dense, a hundred feet above the trees.

'His mother asked me to have him watched over because he is of febrile spirits. He also lacks the social training of a junior school. So I promised his mother I would have him watched over. And as I promised her I would like you to promise me to watch him, and to make sure he comes to no hurt or harm.'

The cloud began to move in a sort of vortex. It was a whirling cloud turning on itself, and darkening as it did so.

'And I venture to say this charge will do as much for you as for him, for such are the mechanics of kindness. That is how it works.'

How far, how very far this was from the mark we shall see.

'His name,' the doctor said, 'is Dynevor.'

The final whistle went. The cloud swept around us, over our heads. It was a flock of starlings filling the sky, a million of them. They whirled round a small copse, and gathered in tightening circles. They went in to roost from all directions, and great hogsheads of birds weighed down the branches of the ancient trees. It was a sinister moment, there when I first heard about the mechanics of kindness.

It is too easy to be unkind

So I was to look after the little Dadaist. Make sure he came to no harm. Make sure nobody threw him out of a window before the end of Governor's Grace. 'At least,' Cavendish said, smacking his lips in an obscurely repulsive way, 'you don't have to put on a rubber apron and soap him in the bath.'

Yes, there was that at least, but I had many better things to do than look after Dynevor. There was something I didn't quite care for in the alert little face, and the thick, sun-streaked hair, and the impudent sway in the small of his back. Didn't understand it, didn't like it.

I am not naturally an unkind person, but it is an easy habit to fall into. Moral sloth may not be a likeable trait in a man, but there it is in all of us, I don't know why. I myself had been treated with terrific moral vigour, and look at the boy I was as a result.

Vigour was our watchword. One of the first virtues, the one after courage. The virtues that made all other virtues possible. Without courage you couldn't be kind, without vigour you couldn't be bothered to be.

And Lord knows it takes energy to make a boy. 'Take your elbows off the table!' you say, and he lifts his elbows an inch off the table. And keeps his hands under his chin. And his friends laugh. They've a limited sense of kinship at that age. They've got no sense of their kind. They have to be taught.

Here's a kinship test for you. There's a right answer and a wrong answer to questions. See if you can tell which is right and which is wrong in this exchange of pleasantries: 'Where is your middle button you oily little tyke? You haven't got one! You are slack! You are inefficient! You are in chaos! You are boiling, boy, with primordial chaos, aren't you!'

Answer one: 'I'm awfully sorry, Fortescue, the fellows were ragging and my button came off.'
Answer two: 'I pulled it off to make the cut of my jacket more individual.'
Answer three: 'Lightneeeng!' (while switching The Pit lights on and off).

'Well produce your Cozens! Where is your needle in your Cozens! There is no needle in your Cozens! Why is there no needle in your Cozens?'

Answer one: 'We were making a blowpipe, and we needed a needle to make the dart hold, please Fortescue.'
Answer two: 'I don't know why there is no needle in this silly little bag, and what's more, the whole concept is puerile.'
Answer three: 'Mama's dead, and never filled my Cozens up! Boo hoo hoo!'

'So where is your needle now, you horrific little tic?'

Answer one: 'Sticking out of Prettiman's backside, please Fortescue.'
Answer two: 'I have the right to remain silent. It's a free country.'
Answer three: 'Doughnuts! I must have doughnuts or I'll never speak again!'

The correct answers are answer ones. The second answers are Robertshaw's. The third – why me? – are Dynevor's. My charge. I looked at him with distaste. Aren't boys awful? Ignorance makes a boy awful, I suppose that's why their parents send them to school.

The row was about a button undone. Tugs were not allowed to undo their coat button (it was a privilege, not a right, to undo that middle button). If Governor's Grace were over both Robertshaw and Dynevor would have been beaten painfully, and probably more than once.

'Come, come,' you'd say, 'It's only a *button*!' Wouldn't you? Don't deny it, I can hear you saying it from here. 'Beaten for a button!'

Well you are wrong. A button is the least of its significance. An unstopped button is that strait route through which chaos comes bubbling into the world.

There is only one rule and this is what it is: if your buttons are properly fastened you are equipped to face the facts of life. On the other hand, if the young infantryman will not fasten his buttons, odds-on he will not make his bed properly. And (it's a slippery slope) sooner or later he will find himself alone in open ground under a malevolent crossfire of professional scorn and enemy sniper-fire. Don't ask why: that's how life works. Learn to keep your buttons correctly done up, and you'll have no trouble with the Inland Revenue. A properly buttoned man will fill in his tax returns, for instance, and have them in on time. He will have no worries in life. He will have nothing hanging over him, no, not a cloud as big as a man's hand. His conscience will be as clear as an African sky.

But you who are now late with the Revenue, your trouble is this. You can't pick up this sense of what is proper in later life. When you've left school you know too much. Experience confuses us. We need to learn things like this when young and untroubled. It starts here. Now. In The Pit. Do up that button. Produce your Cozens. Do not use the occasion to practise your primitive sense of irony. Use the needle you will find there to sew your button on.

The real question is: why didn't we take the little tics out at once and rattle their heads against a locker door, Governor's Grace notwithstanding? That's what *kind* would have done. Kind would have taken the infant's head and rattled it against a locker door. That was the act of kindness, and I am not unkind by nature.

We did not want to hurt him – though that would in some sense have been inevitable – we wanted to show them the importance of respect. That's something we can all agree on, even if we wear our hair in ponytails. When travelling in foreign countries one must respect local customs. Out of courtesy, certainly, but also out of commonsense. If you act without respect, you may have your head cut off and used as a football.

This seems to me to be a valuable lesson to learn, and the kind man is the one who will rattle your head against the locker to help the lesson stick. It is less painful, and less significant to the course of a man's later career to have his head rattled against a locker door than to have it cut off and used as a football. There may be those who disagree, but I stand by this idea of mine.

That is why I marched in to The Pit and told Dynevor to come with me directly. To his credit he followed my gesture and he trotted after me into Cloisters. He held his hands behind his back in an obedient way, but I didn't believe that. I wasn't born the day before. I spoke to him sternly. I wasn't having any of his nonsense.

'Dr de Zoete has asked me to look after you and steer you through Governor's Grace. That is the period of two weeks you have when no-one knocks you about for being thick and ignorant and in chaos. But at the end of two weeks you have to take a test for your Liberties which you will pass or you'll be beaten by an Usher. You have to know, for instance, how many blades of grass there are in Cloister Court. How many do you think there are?'

'Four or five million at a guess.'

'There are three. Not three million, just three. A blade of grass is what we call a lawn here, so remember that. How many tiles are there on Monckton's roof?'

'Gawd,' he said. 'None?'

'Funnily enough you're quite right. Monckton's is on the ground floor, but it's still called a Roof. That's very good. All right. What were the nicknames of the sons of the assistant masters who were killed in the Napoleonic Wars?'

'Coo. Haven't the foggiest.'

I wheeled on him in triumph. 'That's *right*. That's *exactly right*. You haven't, have you? So you don't know everything, *do* you? But you better make sure you do know everything by the end of Governor's Grace.' He looked startled by the strength of my outburst, and I hadn't wanted to hurt his feelings. I said, 'So let's shake hands on it and I'm sure we'll get along, in spite of the difference between us in age and position.'

We shook hands. I led him towards Tollestons where I'd remembered a set of lockers perfect for my purpose.

Perhaps I made a mistake, talking. Perhaps I shouldn't have talked, but I did.

I blame myself.

'Now tell me, Dynevor, I've been doing some research on you. Why is it that your name has Ld before it in the College List?'

'Oh that . . . er, my parents made me into a limited company, you see, for er, tax purposes.'

I didn't like to say I had no idea what tax purposes were, let alone a limited company. 'Never mind about that. Now, Dr de Zoete tells me you haven't been to school before. Why not?'

'I was in Africa. When my father um, when, more to the point my *mother*, I think . . .' he began before I cut him off. I had looked at him again, and I saw that those eyes of his were filling.

'Now look little flea, you little mote of dust, listen to me. When we're alone like this it is all very well to prattle happily along. But I must warn you: in public it is a very different fish. You must remember two things immediately: you must *never* speak to anyone senior to you unless you are spoken to first.'

He became indignant. 'But you did speak to me first.'

'Never mind that. It is vital to remember that older fellows hate it when you *speak*. So if in doubt, remain silent.'

'And the second thing?'

'I'm getting to it as fast as I can! Good grief! The second thing is this: you are not allowed to *think* at Salisbury until you've got twenty juniors. Myself, I shall be thinking next year, but I'm in no hurry to start.' We came upon the lockers at last, and I sized them up while I was talking to him, testing the hinges.

'Why aren't you allowed to think?'

'Trick question, eh? Why aren't we allowed to think? How would I know, Dynevor, unless I'd been thinking? I wouldn't tell you even if I thought I knew the answer, because frankly I can do without the beating at the moment.'

I found out much later that there was a perfectly good reason for not being allowed to think. Because people only ever think about themselves. And you can't think about Little Miss Me, and learn the nicknames of the masters' sons during the Napoleonic wars at the same time. There would be time later on to make sense of everything you'd learned. In all its abundant contradictions. But for the time being you were there to take everything in. So it was a good rule, and best of all, it didn't need thinking about.

'I do say "I think" a lot. Is that awful of me?'

'Appalling,' I told him crisply, and his little face fell. 'But look here,' I went on, for what madness I can't say, 'I'll tell you what . . .' I blame myself, I really do, 'With me, you *can* say "I think" if you like. Until you get the hang of things. But just as long as no-one else hears or there'll be the dickens of a row. All right?'

'Thank-you, that's most awfully kind.'

The word 'kind' put me in mind of what we were here for. Ah yes! I banged the door forcefully.

'Why are you doing that?'

'What? Oh, to see if it will take a certain impact. Just stand here will you?'

'Here? Certainly. You know Robertshaw says "I think" too. He was asked whether he was a Hog or a Peely-Po thing, and he said, "I *think* I'll be a Heely-Ho Robertshaw. Or maybe a Pog Robertshaw." '

I was so shocked I let go the door. He said, 'Shall I test the door for you?' and started to do so.

'Pog! What? Heely-Ho? Who did he say it to?'

'To a goodlooking older boy with black hair, and when he makes his shoulders work, his eyes go like this.' Dynevor's face was moving. It was giving off that thing that faces give off when the internal machinery is working.

As I looked at him closely I felt the whirlpool turn in the back of my head. What did they mean, those flecks in his eyes; the root of each eyelash was visible. Why? It was as if the air were suddenly flush with some psychic musk. I hit myself a blow on the head with the locker door which partially stunned me.

'Great heavens!' Dynevor cried, 'Are you all right? Your poor head!'

'But that's Delavera you're describing!' I groaned. 'He didn't call himself Pog to Delavera!'

'And Heely-Ho.'

I hit my head on the locker door again.

'Do be careful! That must hurt terrifically!'

I reeled away moaning, 'It's not clever! It's not funny! It's simply puerile.'

'Well that's what I told him. It would be clever, and amusing, and mature, Robertshaw, to call yourself Hog or Peely-Po. But you're doing the opposite which is stupid, unamusing and, er, puerile.'

I bled a bit and said, 'What the dickens does he think he's doing here? Why the devil does he think he's been sent here?'

He almost smiled, but his brow lowered. 'It's so that when our parents die we'll be used to it.' His forehead lifted and he looked at me.

I'd forgotten that. When first sent away to school. At the age of six. We talked after lights out, and that's what we all thought. We had been sent to school so that when we died our parents would be used to it. We had been put apart from our mothers – and, I suppose, our fathers too – so that we would all be used to it when we all died. A locker door crashed behind, rousing me.

'I think this door is the strongest,' he said. 'This is the one you would want. Would you like me to stand anywhere in particular?'

There was a moment there when I could have taken him by the collar and clattered the locker door about him. Then the moment passed. 'No,' I said, rubbing my face. 'It's time for Evensong.'

I blame myself.

Oh Lord open Thou our lips

'I hear you've got a Robertshaw in your House,' people shouted out to us as we walked to Evensong. In Mob Quad a group of Foundation Scholars with clever faces; in Hop Quad, three members of the Revel in hunting waistcoats; in Cloisters two choristers. They all asked the same thing. 'Is he a Hog or a Peely-Po?' What can you say?

1) 'Er, what was that? I didn't quite catch that?'
2) 'Er, I thought he was in your house, wasn't he?'
3) 'Er, no we haven't.'

Humiliating. And then that fat little ferret Wheen tried to cut in front of me in Chapel to sit next to Dynevor. 'No you don't, I've got to look after this little sprat. Dr de Zoete asked me to.'

I felt my duties hang heavy I can tell you. The clerical officer reading from the Wycliffe Bible was drowned out by the excited buzz of chatter, and I was stuck in the low pews with the juveniles. I was forced to call over to where my friends were. They had some fun brewing up. Deniston had some gunpowder and a candle. Fortescue obviously had a rat on a fishing line, and here I was stuck with the kids and their silly voices. 'Compulsory religious observance is an infringement of human rights,' Robertshaw said. 'Freedom of association is guaranteed in the constitution.'

'Oh shut up Robertshaw!' I told him. 'I've been asked three times whether you're a Hog or Peely-Po and I haven't been able to tell them, so just shut up *talking* and keep your stupid mouth *shut*.'

He was about to reply and I might have fallen on him with my Beaker People (they hurt, in spite of the missing pebble), but across the way the gunpowder flared, the rat ran and the fishing line squealed. A muted round of applause greeted this as the rat nipped and scratched his way down a line of ankles in the higher pew. You would have paid any money to see it. Funny as a fight. But then

Chancellor started to sing from the choir stalls and a new mood entered the School. Boys are sentimental creatures. I certainly was. 'Oh, for the wings, for the wings of a dove, Far away, far away would I roam . . .' Chancellor's voice soared out of the treble section, spiralling up into the ambitious architecture. Thoughts of violence faded away. The candle was doused. The rat was reeled in. A faraway look came into people's eyes.

Either side of the nave, ranks of boys banked up in the raked pews faced in towards the aisle. Each face a lamp, a magic lantern in the low, ecclesiastical light. Ranks of boys in black coats and white ties. The lines of their shining collars. Candlewax in the air and the scent of old silver drifting like ghosts through the congregation and the chorale.

When people ask whether God exists I say I don't know. I assume he does. But I do know angels exist, I've heard them singing. We were a singing school, but what mystery was in those certain fifths, that minor key. How the treble of a choirboy could play on the reflexes of a public school.

'Who are those boys?' Dynevor whispered. He indicated twelve young ones behind the rood screen. They sat there giggling and gossiping and eating oranges passed them by adjacent supplicants. But even they in the grip of the music sat with dreamy expression, and gently leant against one another like cornstooks.

'They're the College Tarts.'

'Why were those boys passing them oranges with notes attached?'

'They're trying to suck up to them. The oranges will be passed down by fagmasters higher up the stalls.'

'How do they get to be College Tarts?'

'They started as House Tarts and the twelve best are made College Tarts. They sit behind the rood screen to keep them out of sight during worship.'

'How do they start as House Tarts?'

'Oh I don't know. People say, "He looks like a bit of a tart," and off he goes. And then all the House Tarts get together once a year to put on a Smoker, and the twelve top tarts become College Tarts, and they get off College discipline.'

'I see. And tell me this, can you bear it? I so want to know everything about Salisbury: what do they actually have to *do*?'

A word on what modern, so-called academics call 'homosexuality'

Didn't happen. Not in my experience. Not at school, anyway. Different story in the desert, of course, among the Arabs. I assume it was different among the Arabs, I didn't enquire what was really going on under their dhurbas. But a vicar once explained the significance of The Seven Pillars of Wisdom to me. Didn't like the sound of that. Didn't care for that at *all*. Then he kissed me. I caught him a beauty just above the heart and he went down like a sack of meal. Quite unnecessary behaviour in a vicar.

Where were we? The hovering demon? Exactly.

Never fathomed that one. At my kid's school the head man sent me off with the following advice: 'You may find that if you muck about with yourself in the night you can produce a pleasant sensation. My advice to you is this. Don't.'

'Received and understood sir!'

'You may also find that certain senior boys at your public school ask you to go for a walk with them in the woods. My advice to you again is this. Don't.'

Fair enough. Pleasant sensations in the night are out, and no walking in the woods with senior boys. Hadn't the faintest idea what he was talking about then, and as I was obedient by nature I never did find out what the devil he was driving at.

So what's all this about College Tarts, then?

The fact is that a certain sort of glamour hangs around a certain sort of boy at a certain age. You know what I'm talking about, don't act the idiot. Something to do with their flashing eyes, and thick lashes. Hair the colour of wet sand. Faces like cherubs. Skin like . . . whatever skin *is* like. And these boys were called tarts, I don't know why. Always assumed it was something to do with Alice in Wonderland. However at Eton, I found out, they were called bitches, and I never liked the sound of that. It had a cruel ring. Eton, you see; and whatever we were, we were not Etonians.

So, there we had these tarts. Junior ones, as I say, were House Tarts, the more successful graduated to be College Tarts. They would be what was called 'taken up' by established men and given the protection of their status and prestige. Very sensible administrative practice. Tremendous opportunity for advancement. In this way the lowest of college creatures could enjoy the privileges of rank, the advantages of a special education in society, the conversation of his betters, and protection against the attentions of his malevolent contemporaries.

We had many examples of selfless service. Sheba. Devoted to his Tartmaster. An apt pupil. Modest. Diligent. Supervised his master's fags. Ran the study like a high-class hotel. Always oranges in the bowl and a cheerful fire in the grate. No-one knew why he would attend so to a surly and unreliable man (not steady at all, the Tartmaster in question). But Sheba would cajole him into issuing weekly invitations, and everyone came. And when the Tartmaster was treated to a public flogging and was expelled for an unspeakable crime, Sheba shaved his head and wouldn't speak for two years. I think he's in the Secret Service now. That's where most of the College Tarts ended up in one capacity or another.

I never liked them as a matter of fact. All gone a bit wrong by my time. All got out of hand. All that giggling and gossiping, and sidelong glances. Calling one another Susie and Judy, and Alice and Daisy, what's the point of that? And dressing up in petticoats on Saturday nights in full stage makeup to sing 'Three Little Maids From School Are We.' I know it was nothing less than what went on in Colditz, but I felt it wasn't entirely wholesome. I didn't like the way they sat in the Captain of Swimming's lap to ruffle his hair. That wasn't right. And look at the effect it had on national security. No, no, call me old-fashioned but it had all gone a bit wrong by my time.

But then everything started to go wrong in my time

It's extraordinary how *dense* life was in those days, compared with the soup it later became.

Today, people ask me what I did over the weekend. 'Haven't the faintest idea,' I tell them. They assume it's a joke. In fact I can't remember a blind thing that happened between 1965 and 1978. And yet I can recall everything that occurred in the two weeks of Governor's Grace in my second year at Salisbury. Why is this? Am I getting older faster? Or are things speeding up around me? Time, you know, is measured by events. If you measure time in bottles of claret, it goes like *that*, and *that*, at five bottles a day. And the faster time goes, the less there is to remember happening. There may very well be ash on my waistcoat, don't interrupt me.

I remember everything that happened. And then there were the things that didn't happen too. I didn't rattle Dynevor's head against a locker door. You've got a sober, inquisitive mind, why *didn't* I do that?

Cavendish in his armchair was very decent about it. He huffed and puffed and mopped at his face with his big red handkerchief and said the blows to my head had caused a temporary insanity. 'Dynevor can loosen a man's sense of right and wrong simply by pouting at him!' he said.

'It is polite of you Cavendish,' I told him, 'but it is not kind. I fear it was some sort of weakness on my part, no, no, I do, I really do. Some sense perhaps of trying to ingratiate myself to the creature.'

You see why introspection is dangerous. No man's

character can take too much of it. I walked around Mob Quad twice, smacking my fist into my palm. And then I determined to settle the matter there and then. As it happened, I didn't. I had three attempts at settling the matter, one after the other.

My first attempt at settling Dynevor

The tugs in The Pit sensed my weakness at once, of course, like dogs. Loose grip. Lost authority. They knew exactly what was going on, like dogs do. When I swung into The Pit Robertshaw started to tear his hair at his desk and made ape-faces at the College rubric. Pog! Heely-Ho! I resolved to take him in hand there and then. 'Now look here Robertshaw. I don't suppose anyone's spoken to you yet, so I suppose I'll have to.'

'Actually for your information, you are wrong, I've had several people speak to me, they've said "Gravy, please", and "What's your name?" and "Pass! Pass! Pass!", and—'

The Pit was snickering. Dynevor stood behind the ruck with a complicated expression on his face. Moynihan, who was supposed to be running The Pit put his hands behind his head and laughed.

I gestured. 'You absurd boy. You are about to be blown to smithereens. You are going to have to change your tune right now if you want to survive.'

'Oh really? What tune would you like? How about "I've Got A Lovely Bunch of Coconuts"? I can play that on the kazoo if you like?'

You would have knocked him down. You would have thrown him out of a window, or hung him from a beam. But patience is always needed breaking in a colt.

'You spree little twig,' I said pityingly.

'Oh, I say, there's no need to be rude,' he replied.

'Yes, that's definitely rude,' a couple of his supporters

murmured. 'Do people *have* to be rude to get their point across?' My face took on a life-threatening colour.

Robertshaw turned to me. 'It's a well-known fact that rudeness is a sign of a small vocabulary.'

The mob instinct is a valuable instinct, goodness knows we depend on it. But if it gets out of control, it can be dangerous. Damned dangerous.

'I was only making conversation,' he pouted, 'and you shout at me. You bully me.'

'There's no bullying in this Roof!' I fairly yelled at him. I slammed my fist on the table to make the point hold.

'There!' he said to the others. 'Did you see that? You've *just* defeated your own argument.' He folded his hands.

You have forgotten how unlikeable boys can be at that age. How cocky they are. How egotistical. And how bad, how very bad, their jokes were.

In the course of his school career Robertshaw came to exclaim, with an air of bewildered indignation, 'The system is suppressing our individuality!' So conceited was he that he could not hear it when you said 'Of course the system is suppressing your individuality, Robertshaw. That is what it is for.'

How would you deal with a boy like that? Perhaps you think we should have killed him at once and been done with it.

Oh, I don't think so, do you?

No, no, no, you go too far.

You are too severe. You lack charity to suggest such a thing. You have no sense of proportion between crime and punishment.

I refuse to think about it. The blow to the back of the head is an ugly business. The hurried camouflage and the night-time dash from College. There is no kindness in that at all. And as we all relax into the deepening contentment of life without Robertshaw, he begins to disintegrate in a rubbish bag at the bottom of a gravel pit . . . No! That is premeditated murder you are suggesting! I will not be a part of the means to it, however fine the ends! And you lack spiritual knowledge, for murder is a form of suicide, and I would not kill myself for Robertshaw, nor any his friends.

Robertshaw was the advance guard of a troop of youth. Items that expressed their individuality in annoying ways of wearing their hair. Would you kill yourself for that? Perhaps you did, it was a morbid time. But it can't have been all my fault. I'll take the blame for anything you like, but it would be egotistical to take the blame for everything. And there was that consumer boom in California. And those popular musicians that everyone was talking about. And the lower classes were buying washing machines on credit. I don't know why it was, but the whole sense of our common purpose was beginning to disintegrate.

Evidence of this you still see in middle class lavatories. School photographs of the time. Rows and rows of us. Confident, rather brutal faces. But the way we dressed! (The ties took over a minute.) The College Bloods prepared themselves (how shall we say?) like matadors. Like gunfighters. Impeccable buttons. Coats clung to their torsos. Cuffs like blades, no wonder their movements were deliberate. They had the carriage of gentlemen, and a manner when annoyed of glacial courtesy more awful than anger.

But here and there, different sorts of boys. Sullen examples of early dissidents: scowling, doubtful faces looking sideways at you, louche, brushed-forward hair. Boys with unimpressed, ironic expressions. Boys with opinions about things. Boys who said, 'I think . . .' all the time. Boys who were quite capable not only of questioning everything you told them, but who were also perfectly prepared to contradict you outright.

These were the boys who went on to write up their early memories in plaintive satires of the public school system.

I am a man who hates a satire. I like everyone, as we know, but I do not care for satirists. They have contrary natures. Nothing is to their taste except other satirists (whom they generally dislike). And if you have the purpose to, you can satirise anything: 'Thirty grown men running round a muddy field chasing an inflated bladder' (Rugby). 'Two grown men batting a silly little ball against a wall' (Rackets). 'Six hundred grown men dressing up in funny clothes and renting out their privates (the Brigade of Guards). What's the point? You can make anything sound silly. You could satirise the Half Quad game if you wanted to, but why would you want to?

Everything is ridiculous when observed. War, rugby, money, and, I am told, sexual activity. Nothing makes sense when watched with a satirical eye from the touch-line. The Liberties made no sense at all, even to us. But if we were prepared to expose ourselves to the satire of inferior creatures in the process, is it really fair to laugh at us so mockingly for our care?

The Liberties

I was on John, so knocked on the door of the Prefects' Study. Six of them sitting, or standing with their hands in their pockets. Two tugs squatting by the fire making their toast. Mist drifting past the mullioned windows. Clock House tolled the quarters, I was dead on time. Delavera looked up from his paper as I said 'John is going down now.'

'Ah, Wynn-Candy, I hear you've taken a watching brief over the tugs. Good man. How are they coming along? Give us a report.'

'They're coming along pretty well, please Delavera.'

'I mean a report in laborious, wearisome detail, Wynn-Candy. How far into their Liberties are they?'

'They're somewhat into them.'

'This is like drawing teeth,' he said with a smile at his friends. 'Candy – have they got to the John-Go-Down yet?'

'Not yet.'

'Can they shirk?'

'They should be able to shirk, I've shown them how to.'

'And . . . er, Dynevor? Is that his name? He seems a promising type?'

Suddenly everyone went quiet in the room, and I noticed they were all looking at me. 'Yes,' I said.

'You are making sure he doesn't, er, fall into the wrong hands.'

'Yes, I am,' I told him.

An awkward silence developed. Then Norfolk spoke to me. 'Has the tug Robertshaw elected for Hog or Peely-Po?'

'Er, neither, please Norfolk.' I wasn't going to say he'd become conspicuous in the Remove. People asked him whether he was Hog or Peely-Po and he said 'I am Poggly-Po Robertshaw, a piggley-poggley-hoggley-ho, and who, may I ask, are you?' He'd become famous for it, and men came to him deliberately to hear his answer. You know what people are like. Division Heads of the Fierce People came to him (*you* could tell who they were by the thin vertical stripes on their sleeve cuffs – Robertshaw didn't know who they were because he wasn't studying his Liberties). They didn't laugh at his answer, they didn't move their faces at all. They walked away with a frighteningly measured tread. Robertshaw didn't know that tread. He didn't know anything. He was unteachable. During Governor's Grace he was untouchable and as a result he was unteachable.

'Why in the name of Judas is he neither!' Carnahan demanded.

'May be a bit mad,' I ventured.

'The long and the short of it is that The Pit is in chaos, if only Wynn-Candy would say so.' Carnahan appealed to the room.

Norfolk spoke again. 'Candy, I may as well tell you, we are becoming the object of comment in College: The Pit is widely known to be a disgrace. Absolute boiling chaos. We have heard that Robertshaw, far from choosing to be Hog or Peely-Po will call himself . . . a corruption of both these names.'

'Yes Norfolk.'

'Candy. I want you to tell us why you think The Pit is boiling in such chaos?'

'I don't think, please Norfolk.'

'Admirable. Quite right. But you will have observed. You will have observations to make.'

'I've heard Dynevor saying "I think"!' Delavera said.

'For God's bloody sake!' Carnahan cried.

'I better give him six,' Norfolk said.

'You can't do that!' I said in agitation.

'I beg your pardon, Candy?'

'He's still in Governor's Grace, he doesn't understand.'

'I don't think you understand, Candy. We will do precisely as we think best. Be careful what you say next.'

'It wouldn't be fair to beat Dynevor for thinking. I rather said he could think, I don't know why.'

'I see,' Norfolk said. 'In that case I shall give you six. You are not looking after your charge in a responsible way, Candy. Address yourself to that chair, if you please.'

That was a bitter minute then, and it made me limp for half an hour, but worse was to come when Norfolk addressed us all after Absence. 'No doubt everyone in the Roof is aware that The Pit is boiling with chaos. This is not acceptable. We will not allow this situation to continue. It's pure selfishness, laziness and stupidity. We hear that tugs have been saying "I think". So we are going to put a stop to that at least.'

Delavera then reached into his compartment and brought out the awful yellow cane. 'Dynevor, come here.'

Dynevor stepped forward a few shaky paces.

'Have you been told that you are not allowed to think at Salisbury until you have twenty juniors?'

'No! I didn't know! I swear! Nobody told me!'

'You are not allowed to think until you have twenty juniors. Do you understand?'

'Yes, please Delavera.'

'Will you remember?'

'Yes, please Delavera.'

'I am going to impress this lesson upon you, Dynevor, and upon the rest of The Pit. Stand by the block Dynevor.'

The small boy whimpered audibly. 'Moynihan, come out here. As these tugs are in Governor's Grace I hold you responsible for their chaos.'

The Roof watched in the execution-night silence as Moynihan walked up to the block. Delavera took off his jacket. The tip of the cane quivered as he shook it, quivered like the tip of a hornet's sting. 'You tugs are protected by Governor's Grace for the next week or so. At the end of that period you will be eligible for this treatment.' And he began.

When it was over, and the assembly dispersed, Dynevor moved quickly to the bathroom. I heard him being sick.

Moynihan roused himself from his moral lethargy and got to work on the tugs. To hear him you would think everything was going to be all right. But then you heard Robertshaw and you knew everything was going all wrong.

'You awful, bloody, hopeless little bloody oik Robertshaw! You do not say "John is about to leave!" You do not say, "It's time for John to be pushing off!" You say "John is going down now!" Got that in your thick head? That is the John-Go-Down. "John is going down now!" Do you understand?'

'No, I don't understand. I don't understand anything about John at all! *Why should I say it?*'

Moynihans knuckles went white. He was itching. 'You say it because that is what is said. Got it?'

'But who is John? And why's he going off now? And where's he going off to?'

'Nobody knows, Robertshaw, and nobody cares. But when you are on John, you go to Division at precisely seven o'clock and say "John is going down now".'

John was . . . Come to think of it nobody knew any more who John had been, or where he was going down to. It was an anomaly.

'But why do I have to say it!'

'Because we shall have you beaten if you don't.'

'That is *not* a reason.'

'It's the cause then! It's the cause of why you will be beaten!'

'But I am not a parrot! If I can't understand it I can't say it! There's no practical good in it for anyone, *can't you see that*!'

'Shut up Robertshaw or I'll have you killed. Dynevor.'

'Yes Moynihan?' Dynevor was playing up very humble-mumble. His voice low and earnest, his manners ingratiating. He was still in shock.

'How many rounds has anyone fought at Scratch, Dynevor?'

His mouth drew into a rictoid smile of nervousness. He suffered visibly. You would have felt for him. 'Nine?'

'Nine! Nine! No, not bloody nine! Don't you know anything at all?'

'I know how many blades of grass there are in Quad.'

'So do the chimpanzees in London bloody Zoo, you bloody little oik! There were eighty-seven rounds at Scratch, and Peely-Po died! What's the silver called at the Jump Supper?'

'What Jump Supper?'

'What Jump Supper! I don't believe it! Robertshaw! What's the silver called at the Jump Supper?'

'It's called the Jump Silver.'

'Oh well done Robertshaw, clap! clap! clap! You've got one right. If you get one right at Grace you know what will happen to you? You'll get twelve strokes on the block. Twelve! And if you fail the next week you'll get another twelve, only this time with the Sultan of Molucca. What is the Sultan of Molucca, Dynevor?'

'It's the biggest cane in the House.'

'And why's it called the Sultan of Molucca?'

'Because that's where it came from.'

'An inadequate answer! The Count of Medallion offended the Sultan of Molucca, and was sentenced to sixty lashes which cut him in half! Just like you're going to get cut in half!'

'Lay off him Moynihan,' Robertshaw said. 'How can he learn anything if you frighten him to death?'

'Lay off him? *I'll lay off him!*' And with that he took Dynevor's head from the back and bounced it on the desk like a bowling ball.

'Damn you to hell Moynihan!' Dynevor cried. 'You see if I'll learn anything from you! You want to know how many blades of grass there are in Quad? Nine billion. You want to know what the Jump Silver's called? It's called a fart! What's the Count of Monte Molucca? It's nothing! It doesn't exist! And neither do you! You don't exist! You don't exist!'

And with that he fainted.

My second go at Dynevor: he was in bed

He had more than one pillow in the San. He lay among them, one hand, palm up, by his head. Like a Victorian narrative painting: *The Convalescent.* Or *After The Match.* Or, *His Future All Behind Him.* His eyes were closed. Bedded in fresh linen. In the watery autumn sun he looked so peaceful, so young. So untouched by the world. You saw him, and you felt obliged to protect him. He knew nothing. His ignorance, his innocence, he wore on the skin of his cheeks, so . . . delicately.

'Oh hello Candy,' he said softly with an amused tone in his voice. 'I was just dreaming about you.'

'About me?'

'Yes. Would you like to hear about it?'

'All right.'

'I was in a room with someone. And you came in through the door. You wanted me to join the navy, but I managed to get out of it. Then we went out into the stairway. You didn't want to go into the Hall but I made you. It was something to do with saving your life. I made you look into my eyes, and through you went: pop!'

This wasn't the direction the conversation was aimed. I took a grip on myself and asked him 'Have you seen the marks on Moynihan?' He closed his eyes, and then he admitted he had.

'What do you think about them?'

'A fig! A figgle stick. A fickle stick! Excuse me, I'm babbling. I mustn't babble, must I? I know you think babbling is babyish.'

'Look here. What happened to Moynihan will happen

to you if you fail your Liberties. You've got to knuckle down and take it seriously.'

'I know you've got to lecture me Candy, and I know I deserve it. But may I tell you the truth, and you won't be angry? Even though I shouldn't be thinking?'

'Yes, of course you can tell me.'

'The fact is, I don't think I'll ever be able to get my Liberties. There's so much to learn, and it is so terrifically boring I can't get it into my poor thick head at all.'

'That's no way to think, dear boy!'

'So what I was wondering was – can't they make me a College Tart before the test? Because College Tarts have immunity, don't they? You told me in Evensong that they have immunity, didn't you? It would save so much unpleasantness. Don't you think that's the most sensible idea in the long run?'

'Dynevor you chump! They do have immunity, but they don't get elected till the Smoker which is months away!'

'Yes, I'm sure. But for truly special cases . . .'

'Well what's special about you, you little sprat! Who do you think you are?'

He bridled at that suddenly. He told me who he thought he was. 'I am Lord Dynevor! I am the rightful king of Cumbria!'

The rightful king of Cumbria, eh? that cut no ice. At Salisbury it didn't matter whether you were a grocer's boy or you carried a county's name. Not that we had any grocers' boys, but the point holds. You had to take your Liberties. 'A lord, are you, eh?'

'And rightful king of Cumbria, if I could be bothered. But you have to be on time for everything, and they tell you to grow up all the time. I've had enough of it already.'

'That's why you've got Ld in front of your name.'

'Yes.'

'Why did you tell me it was because you were a limited company?'

'It was a joke. As I say, I simply don't have it in me. You know, all the behaviour.'

'Look. Never mind that. Listen to me. You've never been to school before. You pitch up here in your first week expecting to be made a special case of. Not on! Dynevor! You're dreaming again!'

Then he sat up. 'You listen to me! There are five College Tarts who have no business being there at all. Their cheeks are all fat, or their eyes are too small, or their hair's frizzy in the wet, or they've got spots. One's nose is far too long, and another's got a disgusting way of touching the inside of his ears all the time. A *clear five* of them have no business being there. Believe me, Candy, I know about these things.'

'You know nothing, and you understand less. If you don't pass your Liberties, you'll be beaten, but so will Moynihan. *And he won't forget that you caused it to happen.*'

'In point of fact it was *you* that caused him to be beaten. And secondly, I thought you were supposed to be looking after me.'

'What do you think I'm doing you little idiot!' I saw his expression change and added 'I didn't mean that. You drive me too far. I'm sorry but you'll have to take your Liberties yourself.'

'There's something I've been meaning to ask you, do you mind?' His voice was icy. I hated that. He lay pale on his pillows looking at the ceiling with his hands folded on his chest. 'If you are going to be the one to look after me, is there a favour I could ask you for?'

'I have to be the one to look after you,' I said quickly. I can remember my neck getting hot. The edges of my head starting to turn. I had a sudden sense of those starlings turning in the air above the pitch, and the sky darkening. 'I was told I was the one to look after you.'

'*If* you are to be the one to look after me, the favour I'd like is this: you know when you kneel down to say your prayers at night. . . ?'

I did. It was on my list to encourage Dynevor to do the same. A boy should say his prayers no matter what the bruisers say. It brings a sense of completion to the day. And of course it keeps your soul in some sort of order. You don't want your soul lying around like a bucket of spilt fish, do you?

'Could you not do that any more?' he said. 'It's just really awfully embarrassing, because the other fellows laugh so when you do.'

'They don't!'

'How do you know? Your eyes are shut. Prayerfully.'

'They don't laugh. Really? Who does?'

'Oh you know. Those fellows.'

'I can't believe what you're asking me!'

'It's only to be kind. It's not for my sake, it's for yours. You look after me so well, I want other people to respect you.' He was still looking at the ceiling.

'Good grief. Well, since you ask. I suppose I could say my prayers in bed.'

'That would be much better. After the lights have gone out.'

'After lights out,' I repeated stupidly.

'So that no-one can see.'

'I suppose you'll want me not to say them aloud, either.'

'I was going to mention that. But listen. Now I think you should do something for *me*. Just for fairness' sake.'

'You'll have to pass your Liberties by yourself.'

'No. You can get me made a College Tart first.'

'Impossible.'

'Nothing is impossible, Wynn-Candy. Believe me. I know about these things. Shall you come and see me again?'

I suddenly found myself on the other side of the door. I realised my feelings had been stung. I walked out of the San and into College wondering how it was that the little beast could operate on us as he did.

We had all lost the initiative. Not just myself – the Ushers had faltered. The stillness in their study at the sound of Dynevor's name was disturbing. Certain tumblers had fallen decisively into place. We were locked into a way of regarding him that could only end unhappily for all of us.

Realising this, I resolved to put him out of my mind. I

would not visit him in the San. He would convalesce by himself. The end of Governor's Grace was a week away, and a week in that time was beyond the foreseeable future. A week in politics is a long time, but a week in schooltime has the quality of eternity because it never finishes.

And that week did last forever; shortening days under brilliant skies. The winter coming in early, and the cold quickening in the mornings. The scent of coaldust in the quadrangles, and autumn mists in the courts. The flagstones would be frozen in a month, and a bucket of water would make a slide for the Shell. There is nothing better than an ice slide. And in the afternoon, when you ran out over the crackling fields with your friends (what were their names?) the fresh air scythed through your lungs to your vital parts.

Then in the evenings, you walked through College on those early evenings, washed and dressed. Though you may have been alone you had a sense of being among your own kind. Look up into the stories above, and in the windows there was candlelight, and gaslight, and firelight. Boys stood in tall Georgian windows and talked about God or rugby, or each other. Strings sounded from the music school. Small Choir sang, you could hear it faintly in Cloisters. A shout of laughter and a roll of heels on the boards followed a sally at the Literary Society in Big School. A cabinet minister had come down from somewhere to talk to someone.

In the Trading Quarter you could buy food. There was always toast on the braziers. You could buy verses (lines written to order, for your punishment); you could buy items for your Cozens – the Beaker People stones, an ink pot, two nibs, a ball of string, a needle and thread, a ball of wax (no, no idea), and a shilling. They sold you the shilling for thirteen pence. The Trading Posts also produced talented specialists. When we needed a pig, a thirty-seven-stone pig to get drunk and leave in someone's room, we came to one of the Posts and it was arranged.

That was how I came to spend my time in the evening. With Dynevor in the San, and Cavendish in his clubs, I walked around College in different ellipses. You could spend a whole career and never walk the same way twice. You would never know everybody in College. 'You sir, what's your name?' one might say, and the exchange might end in a fight, or a pint of beer together in a room you'd never seen before. Possibly both. The fights were rarely serious but the beer was often strong. You could come across remote sections of College – I once found a group of Empire Scholars who had never been to a common lesson, or played in a match since they arrived (sometime in the 1880s).

The third time I went for him he beat me

In a greatcoat I stood on the corner of buildings, looking down the angles and arches, under the moonlight. Figures moving in and out of doorways, boys in squads, in scads, flowing across the lawns about their business. There were the ravens. There were the bells. And there was a voice I knew in a doorway. There was no light to see, but I knew the voice.

'But I *can* be made a College Tart, though, can't I? I'm told I can't be, but that was only told me by a chump who knows *very* little about these things. He knows practically nothing about anything in fact.'

It was Dynevor in a doorway talking determinedly to a fellow I knew slightly. What was Dynevor doing out of the San? He hadn't told me. He hadn't told anyone. We might have been worried sick for all he cared. The fellow saw me. 'Your pigeon, I think,' and he walked away.

Dynevor moved the edge of his lips sullenly, he sighed and jammed his hands into his pockets in a way we weren't allowed to. 'I was asking him to get me made a College Tart, but he wouldn't help. Why won't you talk to them? I'll never learn the stuff myself, and so I'll be beaten, and I won't be able to bear it, and it will be your fault.'

'Oh I don't know,' I said carelessly. 'I don't know anything about anything, do I?'

He wheeled on me and gripped my arm. 'Don't be ridiculous! I'm desperate! Can't you think of me for a change instead of your own pride?'

'Look Dynevor, being a College Tart is a pretty cheap way of getting out of your Liberties, isn't it?'

He let go of my arm. 'Cheap? I'm taking a cheap way out, am I? Cheap. Me, cheap. I didn't think I was cheap, but I have obviously made a mistake.'

Suddenly I was apologising. Why was that? Why was I apologising? What is it that some people have that makes you apologise when you tell them the truth? Even if it's not your fault? I blame myself.

'Well, you say you're sorry, so I'm sure you are, but it does me absolute zip. So I'll be beaten. I won't be able to bear it. I'll disgrace myself, and anyone who's got anything to do with me, God knows what my mother will have to say about it.'

'What's your mother like?' I asked. It wasn't a question asked at school. Mothers were not like College life. It was rough and tumble here, and arm in arm down the Long Mile with a book of Horace. And the belfry-bag, and the block. Mothers came from another world altogether. They were soft and willowy, mothers were, and graceful, and they moved in a floating way about the house in an evening gown, trailing a cloud of scent and gentleness behind them. And they had hands with long fingers that would cup your face, and look into your eyes without blinking, or laughing, and in the evening when you were all round the fire, she would put her hand on your hair and stroke it a bit. That's what mothers were like.

'My mother is a witch,' he said. 'Like Circe. She turns men into swine.'

'Oh I say.'

'Do you know what men look like when they are turned into swine? The witch hangs her tongue out and goes hagh! hagh! hagh!'

'Do you get on with her well enough at other times?'

He went dreamy for a moment, then revived. We sat on the stone bench outside the chapel. 'If I fail my test I shall run away.'

'You mustn't run away,' I said, too urgently. 'You've got so much going for you here.'

'Oh what exactly? You asked if I'd seen the marks on Moynihan. I tell you, the marks on Moynihan make me literally sick with fear. There's no possible way I can learn what I'm supposed to, because every time I sit down to study, Moynihan's disgusting arse starts up in front of my eyes, and I think there! there! that's what I'm going to look like next week! That's what I've got going for me here: a life of humiliation and loneliness and no friends. Of sitting in Matins looking at five pig-ugly tarts who have noses like this, and eyes like that, and faces like *pizza*, and clumsy fingers and that one with the *ears*! It's just insulting! And I'm going to be cut to *pieces*! How am I supposed to stand it? I can't! I'd rather shoot myself. I'd rather throw myself into a mincing machine and be fed to pigs, and be passed into their digestion to be made sausages out of and be eaten by the Head of Division.'

'Come back, Dynevor, come back. Tell me seriously why you can't just learn the rubric?'

He wheeled on me angrily and stamped his foot. His Italian complexion flared at me. 'Haven't I told you! Can't you listen? Haven't you heard a word I've said? I've obviously turned into the most thundering bore suddenly. I'm sorry. I'll go and be by myself! You obviously don't care about me whether I run away and I'm fed to pigs, or stay here to be cut to pieces. Whatever you promised de Zoete that's obviously between the two of you. That's fine. Excuse me!'

But! Pof! What? Err, hm? Go on! Eh? I mean . . . Well, I mean . . . What?

He surrounded me. Outnumbered me. Outgunned me, surrounded me, shot me up and left me. Left me lying in a pool of guiltiness. Surrounded me in one movement, plunged in the banderillos and left me swaying there with the life running out of my neck. He surrounded me and left me there not knowing what my own name was.

What could you do with such an item? How was one to protect him? If he was left to his own devices he'd fail the Grace. Then he would be severely beaten. Then he'd fail the Grace again and be beaten severely again. And then we would be the object of comment in College. Not only do we have a Robertshaw who claims to be a Piggledy-poggledy-Hog, we also have a potential College Tart whom we have severely disfigured because he can't tell the difference between a Cozen and a John-Go-Down.

'I mean this seriously, Dynevor. I mean this more than anything I've ever said. Running away is never the answer.'

'Yes it is. Running away is a perfectly good answer. It just depends what the question is.'

'The question is: do you have the guts to stick with it and pluckily battle through?'

'A perfectly good question,' Dynevor said. 'The answer is no.'

I do the last thing I can

As an Englishman I really don't like to introduce my friends to each other. Don't think me odd, we're all the same in this. My dislike does not stem from any psychological weakness – I don't worry that different friends may not like each other. What I worry is that you may like each other more than you like me. Suddenly come across the pair of you both having dinner together in a restaurant without me. I can do without that.

It is partly for this reason that I am reluctant to introduce you to Acheson, the grandest of my friends. I only do so because he is dead, and beyond dinner in any restaurant. His adjutant told me he had been run over by a bulldozer. A strange end for a man of his standing. And stranger still, his parents tried to sue the driver for what they called 'compensation'. That was all part of the wind of change, but we'll come to that. As I say, it was a strange end for the Head of Library at Salisbury.

The Duke of Wellington once said that only three men in the world wield absolute power. The Great Mogul. The quarterdeck captain of a man of war. And the Head of Library at Winchester. The Head of Library at Salisbury was the same but a shade more absolute in his authority. You could not, for instance, look at him directly. You wouldn't address him in the second person ('Does the Head of Library require more toast?' was correct). You certainly wouldn't knock on his study door unless your parents dined together twice a week, you had spent all summer putting a new big end into his MG, and he was violently in love with your sister. As this was the case with me, I knocked on his study door.

You will appreciate the state I was in, after the sleepless

night preparing my speech. I ran through the paragraph headings. 'Awfully sorry to trouble you with this – wracking my brains – crisis in House – don't know which way to turn – not as other boys – no social training – Afghan girl by firelight – eaten by pigs – into the digestive system of the Head of Division – *can we get the Smoker brought forward to get him out of his Liberties?*'

He listened to what I had to say. Then: 'I can't understand a word you're talking about Wynn-Candy.'

I started to repeat it, gabbling now, dreadfully embarrassed. He cut me off. 'Do you mind?' I would have said something, but he raised a finger an inch from his armchair. 'You seem to be asking me to *fiddle some private business* for you? I think you have mistaken your man. Excuse me.'

I bowed stiffly, and stepped outside. Things went dark for a minute in the stone corridor. The archways pulsed at the speed of blood. Do you mind? Do you mind? Do you mind? Excuse me. Excuse me. Everything I had dropped in a downdraught of lost spirits. I could have been punched in the face and I wouldn't have noticed. I had asked the Head of Library to *fiddle some private business* for me.

Then I noticed I had been punched in the face. One of the College boys known as the Fierce People felt I'd looked at him, and so he caught me with a powerfully downswinging right. The state I was in I barely felt it, and so fell upon the boy with a sense of relief.

After we'd finished he asked me over to his cell for a pint of beer, and I agreed. 'In point of fact,' I told him, as we got out our Cozens together to mend our clothes,' I wasn't aware I was looking at you. I'd just made a complete ass of myself with Library, and didn't know where I was at all.' In reply to his enquiry, the whole sorry story came out.

Rowse (for that was his name) didn't ask after Dynevor at all, which was something of a first. He finished sewing the thin silver stripes onto his sleeve cuffs (which I noted with awe), and he asked about Robertshaw. 'I haven't believed it myself. They tell me you have a Robertshaw who won't come out. Would you like to come and tell them the whole story?'

I thought of the rumours I'd heard of the Fierce People. One of their number (and not the worst) wore a headband: samurai, kamikaze. They had a depraved raven that had been taught to speak. There were knife scars in the door. They took off their clothes to wrestle in a circle of fire. I said I was sure he could relay my information if he wanted to.

'And what's he like, this Robertshaw who won't declare?'

'You tell him he'll have to change his tune and he says, "Will *I've Got A Lovely Bunch of Coconuts* do?"'

Rowse gave low whistle. 'Not good.'

'He runs up and down the pitch with his arms out like this, making aircraft noises out of his mouth.'

'I don't like the sound of that.'

'You ask him if he's Hog or Peely-Po, and he says he's Piggley-poggley-hog.'

We looked at each other. An awful thought occurred to Rowse which he struggled to put into words 'Do you . . . Is it possible . . .'

There was no answer to that. I left shortly, leaving my new friend with a dark look on his face. We shook hands amiably, and I returned to my Roof.

Dynevor wasn't in The Pit. He wasn't in the bathroom. I walked the length of the Long Chamber and found him leaning up against the shadowy wall at the end of his bed.

'Oh hello, Candy,' he said, swinging his leg idly. 'Did you get to see Acheson?'

I told him what had happened.

'Don't let it worry you, old boy. I didn't expect it to come to anything. We would have been running away tonight anyway.'

I took him by the throat and lifted him back against the wall. He didn't struggle. Chickens struggle when you pick them up, *unless you are going to kill them*. Then they relax, resign themselves to the inevitable. Dynevor went completely limp; only his eyes remained alive. He said, 'Sh! Sh! Sorry, sorry! I didn't mean it!'

'Don't ever ask me for anything, ever again,' I told him.

'I won't! I promise!'

'*Ever again!*' I repeated. As I put him down, I was free at that moment. Marvellous feeling. Everything was going to be all right again, I felt it vividly. As I was about to walk away I said sneeringly, 'And where's your pal? You better get going.'

'He's gone to get some pies from the grubber, for the trip.'

I stopped turning as a thought occurred to me. 'Which way's he gone to the grubber?' There was a quick way and a long way. If he knew his Liberties he'd know which was the right way.

'He's gone the quick way, through that door you showed us.'

'The door I showed you not to go through. Through the Fierce People's House.'

'Well? You said it was the quick way.'

Robertshaw missed Absence. His name was put in the book. He hadn't come back to the Roof by lights out. Dynevor twitched. He nearly spoke to me, but I looked at him so witheringly he lifted his chin, made a *moue* and went back to his compartment. I said my prayers especially noisily at my bedpost, and went to bed.

Robertshaw was found in a confused state underneath a buttress by the Nightwatch. A potato (a small one) had been forced into his person. To be frank, I found that unnecessary at the time, no matter how small the potato. And they'd bruised him, stripped him, dressed him in a monk's cowl and left him tied to a buttress iron in Mob Quad. To be bruised, stripped and dressed in a monk's cowl was enough. The potato was surplus to requirement.

Sometimes they went too far, the Fierce People. They were, as we had mentioned to our tugs, animals. No sense of proportion. Very much a law unto themselves. Rather like the Metropolitan Police.

That, it seems to me, is the value of a public school education: when confronted with dangerous and unpredictable sections of Society in later life, one has an immediate affinity for them. In that – I hasten to add – one knows how to deal with them. As far as anyone knows how to deal with the Metropolitan Police.

He limped into House at 3 a.m. wearing Watch's overcoat. The late-night discussion group round the fireside asked him what the devil he thought he was doing at this time of night, and they were intrigued by his tale. 'And the potato you refer to, the small one, was it peeled? Or was it in its skin?'

'Oh,' he said thickly, 'you don't catch me like that. I am not Hog or Peely-Po, and you can never make me.'

That touched me. I'm a sentimental old fool of course, but I was touched by that. He had courage after all, at his lowest ebb. Which is where courage counts. He had the substance we were after, he just lacked the will to lend his substance to us. I blamed ourselves. He deserved one last effort, and I went down to talk to him after Bells.

'The fact is Robertshaw, you've got a lot of pluck in you. You know you're planning to run away, and I'm not going to stop you. But I want you to know before you go that I believe you've got the makings of something, and I'm sorry – damned sorry – we haven't managed to get it out of you. Here's my hand.'

That foxed him.

He stood there with a variety of emotions playing over his face. His mouth worked. He blinked. He passed fingers over his temple. It was a moment before I saw that he wasn't listening to me. He was listening to the throb in the corridor outside House. 'What they did to me wasn't fair, you know . . .' he began to say.

Then a boy darted in and called out 'They're coming! The Fierce People are coming! They're coming for Robertshaw!'

This created a great effect, not least upon Robertshaw. He paled visibly, leant suddenly onto a bedstead. He looked about himself. His Pit colleagues (a chastened bunch of small boys) looked at their hands. The year above looked at him blankly.

The first of them came in, followed by five of them,

followed by another five. They came in banks of five and stood at the top of House. Their leader put a foot forward and made an insulting half bow to Norfolk. 'You have an oik of a boy. A brat. A runt. A rat of a boy, who won't be told. We've come to help you with him as your Pit won't do the work.'

That was the way they talked. Quite different from the way we talked. It was systematically offensive for one thing, and arranged in impressive cadenzas for another. I was impressed. All right, if you insist, I was peripherally intimidated. All right, all *right*, I admit, I was frightened by them.

Delavera stepped up to them. 'Hold hard, you men are off-ground here, you are out-of-statute.'

Brilliant. Locked them in a legal point. Excellent. Gally them into a jurisprudential pen.

But it only made them impatient. They passed a number of damaging observations on the quality of the spirit in our House. Charges of negligence, chaos, fecklessness; tugs a source of ridicule and contempt. Damaging stuff we were unable to deny. It made us shift uneasily and look at our feet. The leader then produced the largest King Edward potato we had ever seen and began to peel it in one unbroken strip of skin. He said we had not even managed to organise one of our number into Hog or Peely-Po, and offered to resolve the situation by making the peeled item a permanent part of Robertshaw's anatomy.

It was brutally humiliating. It really was appalling. A Peely-Po in House. And forced upon us by outside interests. The potato skin swung from the knife, coiling down past his knees. The expression he wore was deliberately insulting. We had no defence. There was nothing to say.

Then there was a running sound on the boards. Then there was a blur of action. Robertshaw passed by me at speed. He was small but he was fast. He ran with shortening steps, his hands were loose, his shoulders low, he was running in a style. He didn't break his stride as he turned side-on and leapt in the air. He seemed to float like a dancer; he seemed to hang in the air one foot potato-high, one left arm reaching out ahead with a delicate finger pointing, one right fist bunched behind his shoulder. Then Robertshaw hit him fat in the middle of the face and the man went down.

'I am Hog!' he cried with a foot on the man's chest, 'I am Hog Robertshaw!'

And it was true. There he was. Hog Robertshaw. Standing frank before us. Not clever. No hint of irony in it. He was coming out of his eyes at a prodigious rate, like stars do when they blow up. He had leapt from the kennel of his prep-school self and landed on the floor of the Long Chamber as Hog Robertshaw. He'd hung in the air like a dancer and come down as Hog. He'd been a long time descending, but on balance it had been worth the wait.

An exuberant explosion immediately broke loose. Knobkerries. Flying squads. A wedge of tight-head tackle-men, the intruders driven back into the stairwell and bundled out into the night.

When the maul was over the House was laughing and shouting and coming up in thundercloud bruises. Boys were cast in their roles for a theatrical reconstruction of the event (Moynihan took the part of Robertshaw). Every year on that date it was replayed, blow by blow.

At the end of the reconstruction Robertshaw appeared with a bowl of warm water and a towel. He stood up to the fagmaster to whom he would be assigned. The fagmaster (whose eye was cut) looked at the bowl, and then at Robertshaw. He took the towel, dampened it, and applied it to his eye. Turning back to his companions he said carelessly 'Thank-you Hog.' And Robertshaw said 'Thank-you Beamish.' And that was that.

In later years the tug taking Robertshaw's part would ask, 'But why doesn't everyone say "Well done" to the Hog, and carry him around on their shoulders?'

'You've got a lot to learn,' he would be told.

The Pit changed from that day. In one fell swoop. The tugs became quiet and diligent; quick faces and nimble feet. The proper distance, the fencing distance was set between them and the rest of the world. You'd say 'Look here, would one of you go down to Five Acre and pick up Delavera's XV blazer?' and three of them would immediately stand up and say 'Certainly we'll go.' They didn't say 'He's got legs hasn't he?' Or 'What's the point of XV blazers, they're just status symbols.' No, they said 'Certainly, we'd be delighted to do it.' As indeed they were. Because when Delavera said to them 'Sling it on the chair will you,' an intestinal light went on. Lit them up from the inside. You don't understand? You're girls or something. And when College men they'd never met before said to them 'You're from de Zoete's are you? How's your Hog?' Then they'd find a new spring in their step as they said 'He's in *very* good form today thank-you.'

It all took a great weight off my mind. Norfolk declared the following day a House holiday. The Liberties were cancelled. Dynevor never had to be beaten. I was in two minds about that. Both were glad. But one was guilty as well.

He'd got out of it. Typical.

It doesn't take much to ruin a boy. He takes one small but decisive step towards the darkness, and before he knows it, as one foot follows another, he is deep in pitch.

There is a thief among us

There was a strong code of honour among schoolboys, perhaps there still is. And part of this code was the feelings we had about property. We all made free with one another's goods (books, shoes, underwear). All for one and one for all. If I needed it and you had it, I took it. Provided you didn't need it at the same time. My dear fellow. No, no, I insist. The level at which property was considered to be private was low on the list of things: money was considered private property. I never really grasped why money was personal and fruitcakes weren't: there was obviously a lesson to be learned in the fact of Egerton's missing money.

'If we cannot leave a postal order in the sum of ten-and-six on our chests of drawers,' Norfolk explained to the House assembly, 'we have taken a small but decisive step towards the darkness.'

That was why. Small but decisive step into the darkness. We didn't want to take any steps towards the darkness, no matter how small. The postal order was more important than its size suggested. We shifted on our feet and looked about ourselves with expressions of bewildered innocence.

'I don't like general investigations, but we shall have one. Arbuthnot and Debenham will interview every member of the Roof over the next twenty-four hours, and we will all give details of our whereabouts between three and four-fifteen.'

Dynevor came to me in my cell. I could see that he was rattled. His colour was up which suited him. But his manner was agitated which didn't. In a series of nervous questions he established that I had been alone in my cell over the time in question. I asked him where he had been, but he wouldn't tell me.

'I was somewhere I wasn't supposed to be.'

'Where? Half Quad? Up on the leads?'

'No. I was somewhere I wasn't supposed to be.'

'Beatable?'

'Yes, I should say so.'

'Oh dear. I'd say you were a bit stuck, then, if I may say so. In a beatable out-of-bounds during a general investigation. That's uncommonly bad luck. Were you with someone?'

'Well, as it happens, I was.'

'Who?'

'The unfortunate thing is, I can't say. He can't, I mean.'

'Who is this mysterious "he"?'

He repeated, as if to a foreigner, 'I can't *say.*'

'Why not?'

He faltered, and fiddled with himself. 'I . . . just can't say who it was.' The atmosphere changed in the room as his colour came up. It made me hot. It bothered me. 'Look, Candy, you've always been decent to me. Very decent, actually. You've done a marvellous job of looking after me.' He looked at me earnestly. 'You see, the thing is, Wynn-Candy, I don't want to be beaten.'

'Not in the least surprised,' I told him. 'There may be worse things in life, but I've only read about them.'

'Candy—'

'When they're trying to dig a bullet out of your chest, and they have to use a red hot bayonet to do it. That's worse.'

'Candy—'

'Or when Indians want to make you a brave and you have to have those eagle claws stuck into your chest and they use them to hoist you to the top of the teepee, that's worse.'

'I do wish you'd listen while I'm trying to talk to you. What I want to know is, why don't you say you were with me. Then we'll both have alibis.'

'But I wasn't with you.'

'Yes, I know, but will you say you were?'

'But I wasn't.'

'But will you say you were?'

'No.'

'Why *not*?'

'It would be a lie.'

'Oh you're so awfully *good* Candy, aren't you? You're so, so *saintly*, aren't you?'

'I don't see it like that. Actually, if you really want to know, I did tell a lie once and I didn't like the feeling it made afterwards. So I have told a lie, but only one.'

'The guilt got you, did it?'

'The fear I'd be found out. Not exactly saintly, you see. Fear. But I've never told another because of it.'

'Exactly why you'd be believed! Candy, I'm really serious about this. You let me down before, won't you make it up to me now?'

'When! When did I let you down?'

'When you refused to have me made a College Tart. I don't hold that against you because Hog sorted it all out. But you've got to help me now.'

'I, of course, don't see it like that.'

He flared up at me in that confusing way he had. It was very difficult to manoeuvre in a room the size of my cell. 'Only because you're vain and selfish, and never think of anyone except yourself. No wonder you haven't got any friends.'

'I have got friends!' I had to stand up to make the point. He was a devil when crossed, he'd say anything.

'You may think you have, but I've heard them talking about you. You've no idea how much I have to defend you.'

'What a lot of rot!'

'Oh, have it your own way.' He changed again, and abruptly shifted his position in the space available. 'It's just a shame, after what my mother has done, after all she's been through.'

Boys, adolescent boys, don't have interesting emotional lives. There is not a lot *to* a boy. Once he's learned not to boast, not to bully, and which buttons he can and can't do up, then you've got what you need to know about him till he's twenty-one. Dynevor had an interesting emotional life, but then looking back on it, Dynevor was not a boy. He was a girl.

'What has your mother done?' I asked him nervously.

'She's written to a certain mother saying how good a certain fellow has been to me.'

'That's very decent of her.'

'Yes, she wrote a long letter saying at least I was being looked after by one particular fellow. And without this particular fellow I certainly wouldn't have survived my Liberties. And that I owed this fellow so much that she doubted whether I'd ever be able to repay him properly.'

I made a decision. 'I see,' I said gravely.

'Do you Candy? Oh are you sure you see?'

'I'm pretty sure I do.'

'Oh tell me that again!'

'I'll tell you what I'll do. But I want you to tell me something first. Did you take the postal order?'

'On my mother's life, Wynn-Candy, I didn't.'

'In that case, Dynevor, I *will* lie for you.'

'Oh Candy, I could hug you!'

'That's enough of that nonsense. I *will* lie for you *if* you will make me a promise.'

'What? Anything! I promise anything, even without having heard what it is!'

'Don't be silly for a minute, I'm being serious.' He sat down and looked at me with his eyes all wide, in the look I came to learn was his most deceitful. 'What I'm going to ask of you, you won't want to agree to. So let's understand the conditions of our own agreement.'

'I agree. What are they?'

'I want you to start behaving properly.'

'Is that all? Of course I will, I promise completely! I'll behave *so* properly!' He stood up.

I said, 'Firstly.' He sat down again. 'Firstly, you will give all those pins back to their rightful owners.'

'But I'm their rightful owner. They've been given to me.'

'And you will give them back. You are not going that way, Dynevor. It is the wrong way. You will not go courting popularity from now on.'

'All right.' He was sullen. 'All right. I won't care about being popular any more.'

'If you worry about who likes you then you will never know who you are.'

'I *said* I won't care about being popular, all *right*.'

'Secondly.'

'You mean lastly.'

'Secondly. You will make every effort to get into the Roof Second XV. You're perfectly capable of it. You have the kicking ability to get you a place in a College team. I'm not exaggerating: you could represent the College at football, Dynevor.'

'Really Candy, do you really mean that?'

'I do.'

'You're not just flattering me with this amazing possibility?' His eyes were wide again in that way, and his voice too earnest to be real, but I believed him.

'I never flatter.'

'Thirdly and lastly?'

'Thirdly and lastly, Dynevor . . .' I looked for words I couldn't find. 'Your whole bearing is wrong. It is facetious. It is silly. Dynevor. You must in future *act* properly. Because when you act properly people will treat you in a different way, and you will begin to *feel* properly. Then you will end up *being* properly. I can't explain it very well, but Dr de Zoete told me that's how it worked.'

'And that's it.'

'That's it. Do you agree solemnly?'

'You want me to change my entire way of doing things, and get into the Seconds.'

'Yes.'

'You drive an awfully hard bargain, Candy.'

'Those are my terms.'

'I agree to them.'

As we shook hands we looked at each other. I said 'Thank your mother for writing to mine. She will be touched by that.'

'What?' he said, withdrawing. 'I never said it was your mother. In fact it was Delavera's mother.'

He shut the door. And then Arbuthnot came in. A dim, pleasant fellow. Kept wicket for Surrey one season. Went to teach Emperor Bokassa's sons how to play cricket. Eaten by a crocodile in the outfield. Very pleasant, very dim. Perfect person to field a lie like this one.

I told him 'I was here in my cell writing verses for Loppy Ludd from three o'clock to four-fifteen, and Dynevor was with me the whole time.'

'And what was Dynevor doing?'

'He was studying the rubric, to catch up.'

'Was he by Jove? There's hope for us all. Good work Candy.'

A good lie, perhaps (it skittled Arbuthnot). A worthy lie, even.

Here's a paradox: a decent lie.

Experience has taught me something about the paradox that you will not find in books. If you discover a paradox it means something very, very important. Let us consider the paradox of the hare and the tortoise. The race begins, the hare is handicapped by fifty yards. For the hare to overtake the tortoise it must first cover half the distance between them. But before it can cover half the distance it must first cover a quarter of the distance. But before it can cover a quarter of the distance it must first cover an eighth of the distance, but before it can – a sixteenth, and before that, a thirty-second . . . so before it can cover a millionth of the distance between itself and the tortoise, it must cover a two millionth of the distance – do you see how it goes on?

What's the answer to the paradox? Don't handicap the hare? No, because they've done the paradox with a non-competitive hare. In fact, they've done it with an arrow showing that the arrow cannot move at all for the same reasons. Before it can move anywhere it has to move half the distance to it, so it can't move at all.

The answer to the paradox of the hare and the tortoise is this: the way we think about hares and tortoises moving is all wrong. We men of the country know that the hare overtakes the tortoise in a moment, and may a moment later be overtaken by a coursing hound, who a moment later is overtaken by a cubic foot of buckshot from a hunt saboteur's shotgun.

Hares move faster than tortoises despite what Greek philosophers tell us. So what the paradox tells us is that Greek philosophers had the *whole way of looking at movement* completely wrong. That's what paradoxes tell us: we are profoundly wrong in the way we are looking at things.

The world goes on according to its nature, and our thinking about it can make it difficult to see what its nature is. Thinking, you see, can make us idiots. Another example from real life to show the wisdom of the College rule which forbad thinking.

Where were we? The paradox of the decent lie. The paradox would have shown me that my whole way of approaching the problem of lying was wrong. *The whole approach to lying on Dynevor's behalf* was wrong.

Not that it was wrong, as it happened. As it turned out the approach was completely correct in its effects which shows, paradoxically, how useless logic is. To anyone other than one applying for a Chair of Logic.

There was a surprise announcement that evening. It surprised me, at any rate. 'In the matter of the postal order, I would like to see Wynn-Candy in the Ushers' Dayroom after prayers. Let us pray.'

I prayed.

A finger plucked at my sleeve from behind. 'If the going gets tough, you don't have to keep it up,' Dynevor said in the cadence of the prayer.

'We have a bargain, Dynevor. We've shaken on it.'

'You don't have to keep it up.'

'Why not?' I saw a pin in his buttonhole, I didn't know whose it was . . . 'I'm not listening, anyway. We've got a bargain. Get rid of that pin.'

The Roof prefects were assembled in their Dayroom.

They had arranged themselves around the room in negligently threatening attitudes. Norfolk shifted in his seat and looked at papers in front of him.

'Where were you, Wynn-Candy, between three o'clock and four-fifteen on the day in question?' I felt pretty confident: quite apart from the alibi, I'd worked out a stunning proof that I couldn't have taken the postal order and was keen to see it in action.

Unfortunately, as soon as the interrogation started I realised I'd miscalculated. I could say till I was blue in the face that I was with Dynevor, *but I couldn't have Dynevor in to say he was with me.* That wouldn't have been right. And I realised what a pity this was when Carnahan screamed 'Where's the postal order you filthy little sneak thief!'

'Harry, please,' Norfolk waved him down. 'Wynn-Candy, we know you were not with Dynevor. Where were you?'

'Before you sneaked out to trouser Egerton's postal order!' Carnahan yelled.

'Never!' I cried.

'Do you have any witnesses to corroborate your story?'

'No, but it's the truth.'

'Aha!' Carnahan shouted in triumph. 'He says no-one would testify! Why wouldn't Dynevor testify! He's condemned himself out of his own mouth!'

'Shall we call Dynevor in to see what he says about this?'

'This is my story, not Dynevor's! He's nothing to do with it!' I said desperately.

'Your story but not Dynevor's,' Norfolk said, bemusedly. 'Well we agree at least on that, Wynn-Candy. Who were you with?'

'Dynevor was with me through the whole period when the theft could have taken place.'

'We know this to be a lie, Wynn-Candy, and you are asking for severe punishment by persisting in it. We will not be lied to casually.'

'Dynevor is innocent. I testify to it.'

'The question in our minds is: are *you* innocent?'

'I've got proof it wasn't me!' I said excitedly. 'It can't have been me who stole the postal order for ten-and-six. I've already got ten-and-six! What would I want with another ten-and-six? *I've already got a ten-and-six!*'

Norfolk looked at the ceiling. My point was strong, it was penetrating, it was irrefutably logical. But it didn't hold. Logic let me down for the second time. 'We know, Wynn-Candy, that you were not with Dynevor during the time at issue. Your movements are unaccounted for during the hour at issue, and we know you have lied.'

'I was in my cell all the time, and . . .'

'Stop there. I know you to be truthful, and I would rather not see you damage yourself by repeating a lie.' Norfolk was a decent fellow. 'Please wait outside.'

Dynevor came to me as I waited. He had his hands in his pockets. 'You didn't stick to it, of course, did you?'

'Of course I did,' I told him. I couldn't move my teeth, so spoke with difficulty.

He went white. 'But I said. I told you not to.'

'We had a bargain.'

'But I *said.* I *said* you didn't have to if it got sticky.'

'We made a bargain.'

He held my arm. 'Wynn-Candy, tell them! Tell them now!' I said nothing. We had a bargain. 'Oh please, please tell them. I thought they would all know, so I said, I *said* to you don't stick to it.'

'It was a bargain.'

There was a voice from behind The Pit door. It said, 'Faaaag!'

Dynevor being nearest he stepped into The Pit. I saw the way the chairs had been arranged. Norfolk said quietly 'Fag, go to my study, and bring up the Sultan of Molucca.'

Then it was hard to stand up straight. That's when the legs started to go.

I meet the Sultan of Molucca

I don't tell many people this.

As a matter of fact, I've never told anyone this.

I've always wanted to be a writer, and perhaps this is the reason I'm telling you now. Perhaps after this I'll be able to go back to my garden.

Those of you who weren't at school in those days but went on to be condemned to death later on, you will be familiar with the feeling I felt then. Those of you who have been called from a cell at five am and taken into a courtyard, and stood at the foot of scaffold steps, and nudged up them at bayonet-point, you'll know all about this.

The chairs had been brought out of The Pit and were arranged in a semicircle round the Black Prince's Block in the Long Chamber. The Watch had been called to his office.

Carnahan tested the Sultan of Molucca with great, searing swipes in the air as I arranged myself over the Block. This was not the usual sort of punishment in our Roof. So, there was the fear of the unknown, as well as the prospect of pain. The combination was very dreadful.

However, I can tell you one cheerful thing. One of the few things that you may actually look forward to. If ever you find yourself in this position. *The first two strokes don't hurt.* Would you have guessed that? The first two strokes are completely painless. Can't feel them. It's like being shot. You feel an impact but no pain. Being eaten by a shark is a similar experience. The shock is so great that the central nervous system closes down in outrage.

All you feel in the opening instance are the Watch's great hands on your shoulders and, for a while, there is leisure to look about yourself. You can examine the nails on the floor from an unusual angle. Admire the shine on the Watch's boots. Experiment with the whiteness gathering around your knuckles as your fingers grip the metal rail. This can go on, it seems, for twenty or thirty minutes before Carnahan's tread skips towards you. You hear a tearing sound in the air, like an attack jet coming in low overhead, your central nervous system closes down in outrage, and you feel a general barometric pressure round your backward parts.

One!

In Regency times at Salisbury there was a very great deal of flogging. Far more than now. Oh yes, very much more than now. There were three hundred and fifty boys in the school, and four hundred names up for flogging every day. Practically everyone would be flogged once a day. Some would go up twice. An elite corps four or five times. In those days misconstruing a line of Homer was floggable – you couldn't get away from it. Flogged for looking out of the window. Flogged for having a bath. If you were flogged more than three times, you were sent up to the Master to be punished. Which was a flogging. Being flogged was floggable! No wonder you got used to it. As the scar tissue grew you became impervious to pain. It would all have felt much like the second stroke—

Two!

There it is now. Like half a dozen lines of sellotape being stripped quickly from the skin. You can see how one can cultivate an amazing indifference to these matters. The first two strokes don't hurt at all.

That's why they give you nine!

Of course in those days, those days we were considering, those times we were fixing our minds upon, there was fun for all, fun for fun for fun for all. Execution was a public spectacle then, and who does not somewhere enjoy the sight of their brothers being punished? Oh you don't, eh? You are filled with awe and horror? I don't doubt it: you're worried it may be your turn next. So you cover your face with your hands. But you look between your fingers, thank-you Dr Freud, next!

Boys in those days were full of fun. There was no code of silence under punishment to restrict their games. They yodelled in those days. They imitated the dismay of farmyard animals under the castrating knife in those days. The noise frightened passers-by in the town, but put only the least experienced Master off his zhaa! zhaa! zhaaa! zhaaaaaaaaaaaaaaaaaaaaaa! zha! zha!

The third stroke is, stroke is, stroke is, *stroke* is . . . a word with a versatile root. Don't you? Don't you? Don't you think? It is not hair stroked, not hair stroked, not the stroke of a rowing eight, the third stroke charms the latent pain out from under the other two. Draws it out, draws it out, like fish hooks drawn out the wrong way. If fish hooks go in too far you have to push them all the way through, and that's what the third stroke is like: fish hooks being pushed out the wrong way through, and this creates anxiety in the back of your head where the blood is thickening. And this is only three, three, the third stroke, it isn't even half term.

Remember this, remember this quickly, from your Liberties. Lord MacIlvaine. Year after Waterloo. Hired an acrobat to teach him the reverse leap from a bending position. On receipt of the first stroke he went four feet vertical, and how the packed gallery roared. 'Touched a nerve, no doubt, my Lord. Pray wait upon the physician if you prefer,' the Master told him. How the champagne flowed that night. Or yes, or yes, there was, there was Walter Capet, who paid an artist to render a likeness of his Master on that prominent part of his person. And when blocked, and his shirt raised, the Master found his sense of humour wanting, and with the aid of two birches completely removed all traces of the offending affzzzzza-garzzzzasaarrharrghaazhargararzzzzasaarrhar rghaazha rgararzzzzasaa rrharrghaaz hargararz zzzasaa

rrra

aaaaaa

aaaa

aarrrrrr!

The f-f-f-f-fourth stroke lifts you into a new atmosphere where it is difficult to breathe. There is difficulty between the lungs and the stomach. You begin to be sure that you will never be able to breathe again. The lung is collapsing under pain. The veins are thick with heavy fuel. You are drowning in your own internal fluids. You will suffocate as a result, and as a result of that you will die. Thank God! You die!

Come back, come back, come back, it must be nearly over. Let's look on the bright side. Carnahan is not Udall. And this isn't 1650. Or 1300, or 590 AD. Things have definitely liberalised since the sixth century. Things have improved a very great deal since the Wars of the Roses in the matter of corporal punishment. In 1658 you would be flogged for not smoking tobacco. Yes you were, you don't believe me, you were. Tobacco was believed to be a prophylactic against the plague, and the boy caught not smoking after breakfast would be cut in half by his birch-crazed pedagogue. Literally cut in half. Literally sawn in half with timber bandsaws. It was less painful that way.

Oh you would hardly believe the beatings handed out in the heydays of the English public schools. Udall, the master of Eton, flogged a boy beyond endurance. The boy lost his grip. The walls became spattered with digested matter and blood. Udall realised he'd acted improperly and kept an assistant master behind to clean up the mess. Didn't want the servants to see. Didn't want the law to find out either. He did five years for something called paederasty. On his release they made him Headmaster of Westminster. It took an Act of Parliament to limit the number of lashes to forty-eight. No, you wouldn't have wanted to be around in those days. This here is easy. You can do this. This is trivial in comparison. But you couldn't have been flogged during the Restoration. You wouldn't find out anything useful about your personality during a Tudor punishment. Nor did that nine-year-old boy who carried one hundred and forty lashes. Languished in danger for two weeks. Died in the middle of the third. Died. Died. Did his mother miss him? We were sent away

to school so our parents would be used to it when we died. It wasn't common to die of beating but it wasn't unusual either. Boys ran away in those days for fear of the lash. And if they made it home their parents would make them run back to school: 'Running away is never the answer.' Make them run back to school where gaharrgghharzzzz-hhaaaaargahargha
zzzzhhhaaarrghhghaharrgghha
rgahar ghazzzzhhhaaarrghhgha
harrgghharzzzzhhaaaaargaharghazz
zhhaaarrghh!
da!
ah*dah*

I can't take much more of this.

The central nervous system that had once closed down in outrage has rallied. I am like the root of a tooth flayed in a sandstorm.

I don't think we need any more of this. On consideration I am now certain of it. More would be redundant. Is that nine? Is that twelve? It is enough. 'Twill do. 'Twill suffice. 'How many's that, Watch?'

'Oh, excuse me sir,' he said, 'I was miles away. Three or four I think.'

Have you ever had the experience of extremes, to notice how it affects your vision? The shine on Watch's boots, for instance, has dulled. That's interesting isn't it? It is as though the world has receded. It is the same with the ears. Your hearing goes too. Carnahan's steps behind are indistinct but there there there there there is another blow, that much is certain. Yes, that was another blow. It felt like a car crash. Like a vast impact and shards of glass flying through your interior; stripping the flesh from your feelings in a storm of flying glass. The stomach has turned to a sort of poisoned gelatine. The brain, however, has slipped its clutch. Fly wheels are spinning in the centres of pain, but we are not getting anywhere. Things are obviously going on, but the effect of them is diminished. What can we be glad of now?

Let us be glad that this isn't a birching where the

executioner lays down the worn instrument, the buds on the twigs dulled from the thorns they were. Nor that he picked up a new weapon, as King Saul had. Was it King Saul? Laid down his exhausted birch and picked up a flail of living scorpions. I will chastise you with scorpions! With scorpions! Ha! Not us, though. At least, not me. I am not being chastised with scorpions. So let us be calm, be careful. Can we be careful?

We can be quiet. Shh, be quiet. Hush, be quiet there. Because at the bottom of pain is knowledge. And the knowledge is this. Pain does not, in fact, exist. It is in the mind. It is merely a mental phenomenon. Just a part of the shadowplay of human illusions. This makes things easy to cope with suddenly. Because there is always a solution to a mental problem. If pain is in your mind, and you cannot bear the pain, then you must leave your mind.

Sh. Hush. Sh. Leave it . . .

easily,
go easy.
Slip the moorings and let go on the tide, it's
easy.
Sail (whoooosh)
away
sssssssail (shooooooo)
sail
hup! two-six hup!
bye bye!
away . . . (*away)
away . . . bye!
away . . . (*out*out*!)
When . . .
your . . .
heart . . . (hahahahaheart)
feels as weary as a w—
as a w—
as a w— (*away)
Wa horn
o u t whoop! Whoop!
glove

Horn
Horn
horn
Sing!
Pull!
(Fire!)
Sail (The sheets!)
away (Fire down below)
sail (There's fire down below) O
away (Fire!)
Ooooo!oooo!
You bbbbttr tk th fr srsly 3!3!3!3!3!3!
1) Yu bttr @) tk 3) th
*) fr
?) srsly
1
Dnt y? *&&&? 'Or nt?' "==++///######

"__________"
"+"
*
*
* * * *

let us urgently consider the question of the fire.
1) Your house has been set on fire by enemies.
2) You can't live here any more.
3) You must get out.
4) Craw out, then. Get out.
Go on, get up,
get out
on to the roof.
Go into the corridor and find the door to the roof . . .

It's dark in the corridor but there is a pool of light splashed on the flagstones. There is a boy in a gay waistcoat standing in the doorway. Who is he? 'You sir! What's your name?' He doesn't answer, but smiles and turns aside. You follow him. When you turn the corner he is gone. Did he step into a doorway? You step into the doorway too, but he is not there. That's odd because you know the door, and the corridor. You know enough not to go in the doorway. But then you hear a treble voice laughing. It is a familiar laugh. You know the laugh from behind the door. So you lean on the door to go in, and when you do, you say:

'Hello Dynevor.'

'Hello Bunter,' he says. And the light in the room throbs, though the room is steady.

'You have strange lights in your eyes, Dynevor, has anyone ever told you?'

He was sitting on the knee of the Captain of Swimming, ruffling his wet hair. 'You are a fool, Bunter,' he said, 'You are foolish to look into my lights. I don't show them to people like you. What business have you seeing them?'

I said 'Why not?' I wanted to know.

He said 'I'm the fool for showing you. You don't want *me*, you fool. I know you don't want *me*. You want to make me into your your *fool*. You want to make me into your *midshipman*.'

'What's wrong with being a midshipman?' I asked him.

'What's wrong with being a midshipman?' Suddenly he was angry. The flecks in his eyes glowed. 'Apart from being shot? And mutilated? And being torn apart by shattered masts? And swept overboard? And being hanged by idiots, and drowned in bilgewater, and burned by Chinese fire, and crushed by cannons coming back at you, and being cooked by cannibals, and being cut in half by pirates, and eating weevils, and getting skin diseases, and having your leg sawn off by surgeons, and living with filth, and being keelhauled and having all your skin and all your muscles ripped off by barnacles and coming up looking like *hell* . . . these are probably advantages unavailable to the most famous College Tart since Sheba – who was a *pig* compared to me, Bunter, a *hog* compared to me. But that's why I am not a midshipman.'

'What are you then?'

'I am beyond Sheba, Bunter, that's what I am, if you can understand it.'

'You're not!' I cried to him, 'You're not! You're not!

you will not be! We have a bargain!' And in my saying so, he disappeared.

Pof! He was gone. There was nothing there.

In the darkness he left behind, in the emptiness he left behind, I was back in the Long Chamber again, with a view of the floorboards, just in time for the full force of the stick to come in with annihilating effect.

hnk! hnk! knk*!*! ssssssss!
hnk!hnk!hnk!hnk!! *!*!*!*!*
,

ssss!——————hnk! hnk! hnk!
!*!*!* wt!wt!————++
sssssssss!——————+++++
++++++++++wt! wt!wt!wt!wt!wt!
,

####&+++ +++++++'+++ +++++++ +
//————————————————+
,,,

X————————————————
————————————————

???''''''

hnk!hnk! hnk*!*! ssssssss!
hnk!hnk!hnk!hnk!! *!*!*!*!*
,

sssss!——————hnk! hnk! hnk!
sssssssss!——————+++++!*!*!*!*!*
,

####&+++ +++++++'+++ +++++++ +
//————————————————+
,,,

X————————————————
————————————————

XXXXXXXXXXXXXXXX
XXXXXXXXXXXXXX
XXXXXXXXX
XXXXX
HNK!HNK!
!*!*!

That's when I disappeared too. I went into the darkness and the emptiness.

I was nowhere.

No I wasn't. He was there again. He was sitting on the lap of someone I recognised twenty years afterwards; someone in some government, somewhere, someone who had to resign from . . . it's not important.

'What's the matter with your face?' he said. 'Have I said something?'

'What do you mean?'

'Your face went in a funny way when I was watching it.'

'I felt something, I think. Like a twist somewhere. Like someone squeezing me somewhere – somewhere that I didn't know about.'

'You are being flogged elsewhere, and you are taking it badly.'

'It's not as bad as you think, young man,' I told him. 'It's medicine you haven't got the guts to take.'

As I said this, I saw a curl develop in the corner of his mouth. He became fainter, and the room started to fail. The Minister started to laugh. I had a feeling in my body like distant bee stings. My whole !!!!!!!!!!!!!!!!!!!!!!!!! body had been !!!!!!!! stung !!!!!!!!!!!!! by huge bees !!!!!!!!!!!!!!!!!!! but my body was so far away I hadn't felt it yet.

Dynevor's face changed for the better. 'Psst!' he hissed. He was close to me, but his voice was strangely faint. He called to me across the gap of inches between our faces. 'Look at the lights, Bunter,' he called to me. 'I have lights in my eyes, can you see them? You can see the lights in my eyes, can't you? Look at them, Bunter, I'll make them bright for you, look at them . . . you can see them now, can't you?'

'Don't call me Bunter,' I said.

'I'm glad you've come back. You are an ass you know, but I can't help liking you. Come on, I'll show you.'

'Show me what?'

Dynevor hopped off the man's lap. Putting his hands in his pockets he led the way through the arched doorway onto the crowded staircase. Boys flew past us in their gowns. There was something odd about them, and not just their collars. We joined an eddy of the mob and went down into Great Hall. Fags scuttled across the flags carrying coal in their Commoners' gowns. The Half Quad game was in full swing. A brilliant sun lit up the ivy-clad walls; not a breath of wind; the ravens hopped about. Then I realised what was odd.

'Who are these boys?' I asked Dynevor. 'I haven't seen a face I know.'

'Oh, you've seen their names on the memorial boards,' Dynevor said. 'You probably learned them for your Liberties.'

'This is before my time, isn't it? What are we doing here?'

'There's nowhere else to be, Bunter, just now. Unless you'd rather go back to the Long Chamber? Carnahan isn't finished yet you know.' He arranged himself on the steps, watching a group of Foundation Scholars leaning against a wall. 'Look. Do you know who that is?'

I didn't. At the centre of the group stood a striking boy with long golden hair swept back from his face. He was spinning a coin idly, and his features moved in a leisurely acknowledgement as his friends around him spoke. He said something in Greek and everyone laughed. At their laughter he made a gesture with his mouth.

'He's *very* good, don't you think?' Dynevor said softly. 'The way he looks at one, and then another, and then doesn't look at the first one. The timing is marvellous. It's a rhythm. He's got them all in the palm of his hand.'

'Who is he?'

'You remember Sheba?' I did. 'That's his grandfather.'

'Where are we? How did we get here?'

'You've run away, Candy. It's never the answer, but here you are. Do you want to see something, now you're here? Shall I show you something? Look at me for a moment.'

I looked at him. The flecks in his eyes started to glow and I went odd again. I felt very peculiar. As in a dream I felt connected with the invisible world, I was in touch with things far away and long ago. There were vibrations travelling down long wires and resonating in the box of my brain. I heard India coming in on the wires. There were Viceroys. There were Vikings coming up the Thames with their round shields. There was Robin Hood, there were Roundheads in the great smoking city, there were the outside jakes in 1939 with bomber squadrons flying overhead through the same shining skies that Arthur saw and hawked in, in the same air Harold knew. And was there still for tea the smell of burning teacakes on the breeze?

This made me shine; I was alight from the inside.

'Oh, you're one, all right,' Dynevor said, 'you've got it bad. Come along this way.'

I became aware of a tunnel. There was darkness all around, but at the end of the tunnel there was light. I went into it. In a moment I found we were in a wood. We walked down a path. There was a stream running in the dark, and we were making for the headwater. Then there was a clearing. Naked men chanted together in a low chorus. After a while I could make out the words. 'Hun gun don' they seemed to say. 'Hun gun don. Hun gun don.' Luckily they couldn't see us. We stood by two crossed oaks, behind a bush of briars.

'What are they saying?'

'I thought you of all people would know that.'

'I don't understand.'

'You'll work it out.'

'Who are these people?'

'I don't know their names. But England is still connected to Europe by a land bridge.'

The men stopped chanting, and a boy was brought into the clearing. They took a length of rope with three pebbles knotted into it. One put the rope round the boy's neck, with the pebble at his adam's apple, and tightened it. The boy struggled, and then died. 'Hun gun don, hun gun don, hun gun don,' they said.

'What does it mean?'

'Loosely? "We have to kill the young among us, so that

we can live." Or it may mean "We have to die as boys so that we can live to be old." It's ambiguous.'

'Why should I of all people know?'

'Guess what time it is. You can't. I'll tell you. It's exactly seven pm . . . You still haven't got it, have you?'

'No.'

'It's the John-Go-Down. Don't you recognise it? John is going down now. Never a truer word was spoken.'

'It seems to be very cruel,' I said.

'You're not going soft on me are you?'

'They killed him.'

'We must die in order to grow old.'

'I don't like it.'

'Do you want to go back now?'

'Is it time?'

'Yes. It's time.'

Everything went dark again. The next thing I knew, they were peeling me off the block like a blood-soaked bandage and taking me to the San.

And then I had him after all

They were very decent about it, all told.

They hadn't ever thought I took the money. Norfolk said so when the postal order turned up in Egerton's sock drawer. He said it hadn't ever occurred to them I'd taken the sordid little thing. It was the lie. That's why they'd put Carnahan to the action.

In my cell, an hour afterwards, after the doctor, I stood thoughtfully. Not that I was thinking. There was a knock at my door. I said nothing. I lay low. There was nothing inside me to say. I was stripped clean inside, like a rifle bore. I was as bare as the walls of the Long Chamber. I was empty as a vault. I was a vault with dust motes circling in shafts of sunlight. I was probably in shock. Yes, that was it. I was probably in shock.

Then he came in. 'Why didn't you tell them?' he asked in the small voice he had.

'I didn't tell them,' I said.

'Why *not*? We agreed what we would say!'

'We had a bargain. You don't chuck them.' I hadn't looked at him at all. Not a glance.

'Are you all right, Wynn-Candy? Did they hurt you very much?'

'Oh, you know.'

'You big ape! They did! They damaged you!'

'Did you . . .' I began to say, but then stopped. I'd been dreaming. I had dreamt we'd been together. I'd had a dream about a corridor, and a doorway. And there was a way through the wood. And then there was a boy in a clearing with the Beaker People round his neck. His legs twitched and went still. I tightened my grip. 'I kept my side of the bargain, now you must keep yours,' I said to him.

'Why didn't you *tell* them?'

'Because we had a bargain.'

'Are you trying to tell me you went through that for my sake?'

'Yes.'

'I don't believe you.' He passed a fretful hand around his temples and I knew I had him. He tried to speak twice before he said 'No-one has done anything like that for me before.'

I gave an extra twist to the cord. 'I don't want to hear, Dynevor.'

He struggled, but I was too strong for him. I was dead. At any rate, I was too dead for him. He couldn't defeat me. You can't defeat a dead man, in my experience. He turned his eyes at me but I just looked away. Then the light went out of his look. He took off the last pin in his lapel and said 'I will keep to my side of the bargain, Wynn-Candy.' And we shook hands. He turned to leave.

At the door I called out to him: 'Listen to the John-Go-Down. Listen to it, will you?'

He nodded slowly and turned away.

I looked at the pin and recognised it. It belonged to Delavera. I threw it in the bin.

Dynevor kills himself

'In my view,' Cavendish said, mopping his face with his characteristic handkerchief, 'Dynevor is to blame. He should be stripped and tied up by the wrists from a beam, and whipped until the weals come up on his body like earthworms!'

Very loyal of him you will say, but I always thought it odd when Cavendish had one of his turns. Still, he became one of the youngest judges in the High Court so he can't have been as odd as all that.

I wasn't angry with Dynevor. I was merely disappointed. My standing in House had gone up (a glass of brandy in the Ushers' Dayroom) and I was admitted to a very select club as a result of my experience (we once all had dinner in Dar-es-Salaam). Admittedly, there was a large, empty space inside me, caused, I assume, by the force of the experience. This made any strong feelings difficult. Fortunately, life was constructed in those days such that you didn't need to feel strongly. If your habits were sound you would be carried along by the strong feelings of others.

And Dynevor was helping. He didn't sulk. He pitched himself into his new role with a surprising debut at our Jump Supper.

In the absence of anything to tell you about myself, let us consider the Jump Supper.

This was a feast peculiar to de Zoete's. One of us had been running from the town mob across our water meadow through a storm. The Flemish engineers hadn't worked their magic on the land. Our scholar leapt the storm water ditch; two of his pursuers failed and were swept away. The Jump Supper was held after the service to commemorate the souls of the drowned. There was beef, and beer, and turns from the tugs. 'Three Little Maids' was popular. The affair was said to be a run-up to the Tart Smoker, so all the bookies from the Trading Posts were there, and the event was eagerly watched by College.

I didn't like that.

But I did like this: Dynevor declined to sing 'Dear Little Buttercup'. The prettiest tug of the year always sang 'Dear Little Buttercup'. The lewd and the loathsome sang along, for reasons of their own, using the words 'dear little buttocks-up' for the proper lyric, I don't know why.

So there we were. The trestle tables were two inches of oak with a quarter inch of polish. There was the Jump Silver. Large bowls of it on each table. Musicians played from the gallery on instruments of the period. Dr de Zoete presided from a stage, a place laid for one. Each of us had invited one from another Roof and we served our guest from the Jump Silver. The fire in the hearth was deafening. Shoulder to shoulder we thumped our mugs. We drummed our feet.

'Here comes your little Dynevor, what's he going to do for us?'

'I suppose it'll be "Dear Little Buttercup",' I said as the hall started to drum its heels on the timbers. The company was captivated by the diminutive figure. He was more sober than they had been expecting. But even in repose his features drew every eye. How did he do that?

'*Dear* little buttocks-up!' a fool shouted as he took up his position. 'Top tart! College Tart!' others shouted. There was laughter; heels on the boards. ' "Three Little Maids!" "Three Little Maids!" ' 'A case of oranges for "Three Little Maids!" '

It did not distress him, he rolled his chin away from the voices, and said:

'This happened in a battle to a battery of the corps
Which is first among the women and amazing first in
war . . .'

'First among the buttocks-up!' one of the voices yelled,

but he yelled it into silence and it sounded thin. Suddenly there was silence. How do people like Dynevor create silence when they want?

'And what the blooming battle was I don't remember now
But Two's-off-lead he answered to the name of Snarleyow.'

Norfolk, at top table, said without interrupting 'What is Two's-off-lead?' and Dynevor replied without pausing 'Two's-off-lead is the left-hand horse pulling number two gun carriage.'

'Continue.'

'Down in the infantry nobody cares.
Down in the cavalry, Colonel he swears.
But down in the lead with the wheel at the flog
Turns the bold bombardier to a little whipped dog.'

He dropped his voice for the last two lines. There was no feeling in his voice: he was factual. It was information he was giving, with the same sort of spinning deliveries that newscasters today bowl down at you: bombs and babies dying, factually, factually. Dr de Zoete looked down for a minute, and put out one of the cigarettes he was smoking for a moment. Did he think the kid knew what it was to be a little whipped dog? Dynevor hurried on.

'We was moving into action, we were needed very sore,
To learn a little schooling to a native army corps.
We had nipped against an uphill, we had tucked agin a brow,
When a tricky, trundling roundshot gave the knock to Snarleyow.

We cut him loose and left him. He was almost tore in two,'

How can I describe the delivery of that awful line? The infant didn't pause for emphasis, but he lifted the pitch of his voice without lingering; he eased away from the T's without trying for any effect. The line was the more awful: 'He was almost tore in two . . .'

> 'But he tried to follow after as a well-trained horse should do.
> He went and fouled the limber, and the driver's brother squeals,
> "Pull up! Pull up for Snarleyow, his head's between his heels!" '

Ahhhh! His head's between his heels . . .

> 'The driver humps his shoulders for the wheels was going round
> And there ain't no Stop Conductor! when the battery's changing ground.
> Sez he, "I broke the beggar in, and very sad I feels,
> But I couldn't pull up, not for you, your head between your heels."
>
> He hadn't hardly spoke the words, before a dropping shell,
> A little right the batteries, between the sections fell.
> Before the smoke had cleared away, before the limber wheels . . .'

(He did emphasise the word 'limber'. The vehicle connected in the middle by a ball joint, like a leg, like a limb . . .)

> 'There lay the driver's brother, his head between his heels.'

You know what boys are like, sentimental creatures as we know, they feel these things. Dynevor's face had an odd, a very odd light in it now. He showed his eyes to everyone, not just to me.

> 'Then spake the driver's brother and his words was very plain,
> For Gawd's sake get it over me and get me out of pain.
> They saw his wounds was mortal, and they judged that it was best.

So they went and drove the limber straight across his
back and chest.'

Dynevor became invisible. A surge of tears that blocked the House's vision. They had driven the limber straight across his back and chest. It is a terrible world. Great and terrible.

'The driver he gives nothing but a little coughing grunt,
But he swung his horses handsome when it came to
Action Front!
And if one wheel was juicy, you may lay your Monday
head,
'Twas juicer for the niggers when the case began to
spread.

The moral of this story is plainly to be seen.'

And his eyes came to rest on mine as he said these words; he found my eyes in all the hall, and held them.

'You haven't got no family when a-serving of the
Queen.
You haven't got no brothers, mothers, sisters, wives nor
sons,
If you want to win your battles go and work your bloody
guns.'

He held my eyes with a level, steady look. The almond-shaped eyes with the thick lashes and the darker-than-sandy eyebrows standing out of an olive complexion that presented his smooth, smooth cheeks. And the eyes, ah the eyes . . . The eyes suddenly went out.

'Down in the infantry nobody cares.
Down in the cavalry, Colonel he swears.
But down in the lead with the wheel at the flog
Turns the bold bombardier to a little whipped dog.'

In the roar that followed, there in the hall, and later in the College sensation, Dynevor became a new person. I had him. The flickering, swirling feeling that his eyes made a fellow feel: all gone. Extinguished. Gone for good.

'My God,' Cavendish said, 'The silly little tart. He's committed suicide in front of our eyes.'

And so I took the responsibility of him. We looked after one another in those days, and life was kinder then.

Pilgrim's Progress

In the street, Marilyn Monroe was said to be able to disappear at will. She'd be walking along inconspicuously, she'd say to her friend 'Shall I be her?' Then she'd turn on the internal machinery, and the traffic squealed to a halt. 'It's Marilyn Monroe!' they gasped. She'd switch the machinery off and the traffic would start again. 'Could have sworn that was Marilyn Monroe,' they'd scratch their heads uncertainly.

So it was with Dynevor. He turned off the lights in his eyes and he became ordinary. Whereas this made Marilyn Monroe invisible it had the opposite effect for Dynevor in the Ushers' Dayroom. It made him ever more conspicuous. Life is unpredictable.

'The boy's an obvious tart!' Carnahan screamed. 'Look at him! Look at him! Haven't seen a tart like that since Sheba! And what does he do? He funks the Smoker! Ducks it!'

The new Dynevor had, on my advice, scratched his name from the running order of prospective College Tarts. All that lay in his past. Did they admire his discipline and self-denial? If they did they expressed their admiration ambiguously. 'You've got no spirit in you Dynevor, you're a worm! We all thought you were a *trick*, but you're *not*. We thought you were a *card* but you're *not*.'

He became listless and depressed. Yes, there was at least that. It was, at least, an improvement on the way he'd been before. No more 'Please, oh please, oh say you will', or 'Make me some toast!' or flicking the switches and going '*Lightneeeng*!' Some people are simply better off depressed.

You may be thinking that I deserved a certain amount

of recognition in House for my achievement. I wasn't doing it for recognition, of course, but even so I was surprised by the general reaction. The phenomenon was treated with caution by all the Ushers except Carnahan who treated it with a wild revulsion. 'Who in the name of Satan does the little oik think he is!' he said more than once.

He coached Seconds and, whenever he had a chance, he hurt my boy. There was no need for it. In tackle practice he'd run straight at him; straight at him, and straight over him. Dynevor, who had no appetite for the tackle took to rolling himself in a ball prior to contact. 'The way a worm goes about it! Wriggling pathetically on the ground. All right, Dynevor, if you won't tackle me, I'll tackle you. Start running for the line!' It is awful to see how a boy crumples on impact. Especially when you can tell he doesn't like it.

I found him with his book walking the Long Mile, an avenue of polled oaks. Leaves scuttled across the flagstones and there were marvellous, scoured clouds racing across the blue sky. We turned our backs to the wind. 'Look here, Dynevor, it's awful the way Carnahan tramples you, I hate watching that. Won't you tackle him?'

'I can't tackle, please Wynn-Candy. I'm doing the best I can, but I can't tackle.'

'Why not? It's easy. You go in at the knees with the shoulder like this. You get down here and then drive in hard at the knees, and your man goes over your shoulder. It doesn't *hurt* if that's what's worrying you.'

'Please Wynn-Candy, I find it hurts terrifically. And also it is very frightening.'

'But, little thing that you are, you must tackle. Don't you see Carnahan has got it in for you because you won't tackle?'

'Please, Wynn-Candy—'

'And stop saying "Please Wynn-Candy" all the time. It's not necessary while we're alone. I'm trying to think of some practical solution to this. How are we going to deal with Carnahan?'

'Deal with him? It would be all very well if anyone could *deal* with him.'

'Buck up Dynevor! We could deal with him in any one of a thousand things! We could get a pig drunk and put it in his room.'

'The *reason* Carnahan has it in for me is because I won't go in for the Smoker.' He became animated for a moment, like Marilyn Monroe. Traffic slowed to a halt in the avenue. The back windows of Big School gaped at him. Clock House stopped.

I said 'Oi! Stop that!' and traffic resumed. I tightened my tie (already at throttling point). 'So your theory is, it's the Smoker, is it?'

'Obviously it's the Smoker.'

'Not because you're gutless.'

'No.'

'Not because you wriggle worm-like at his feet during tackle practice.'

'No.'

'It's because you won't go in for the Smoker.'

'Yes.'

'But we don't want you pitching back into all that sort of kit, do we?'

'I shouldn't mind in the least. I'm just trying to keep my end of the bargain.'

'And don't think I haven't admired you for it,' I said quickly.

'I don't think anything, I'm not allowed to.'

'No need to be like that. I'm not allowed to think either. I'm not thinking, I'm admiring.'

'Well thank you very much. That makes it a lot easier,' he said.

'Does it? Really?'

'No. Not really.'

We were at an impasse. 'I say, there's Cavendish. I wonder if he's got any thoughts. He's got twenty juniors.'

My friend's agile intellect swung into action once the facts had been laid before him. Amazing mind he had. He swung from one idea to another like a liana-artist in a jungle film. He was clever, but I'm one of those peculiar people who doesn't mind that. 'Firstly,' he said, 'Carnahan hates little Dynevor here.'

'Not *hates* him, surely?'

'A writhing, slithery, spineless little worm, who should be hung up by the wrists and whipped, whipped, whipped, till he squeals.' Cavendish's handkerchief was in play.

'I'm not courting popularity, at least,' Dynevor said.

'Carnahan wants a College Tart for our Roof, and he is angry – indeed *personally insulted* – that Dynevor refuses to cooperate.'

'Cavendish is quite right, we're not using our heads.'

'We're not allowed to!' Dynevor said, intemperately.

'Oh for heaven's sake, buck up, Dynevor! What do you say, Cavendish?'

'I say he's marvellous when he's angry, and I think you should release him from that bargain thing you've got him under.'

The far parade of College buildings looked particularly solid. Like a fortress, like an arsenal. I felt my colour rise. 'Never! No! That's out of the question.'

'Then what I suggest is this. Dynevor will go in for the Smoker, to satisfy Carnahan, but we fix it so that he doesn't win to satisfy you.'

'Now that's what I call thinking! What do you think of that, Dynevor?'

'I think nothing. I am thoughtless.'

'He's been like this ever since the Jump Supper,' I told Cavendish. 'But listen: how do we fix it so he fails? No-one else would win if he was up.'

'Tell me, damaged little sparrow that you are, who are the main contenders?'

Dynevor took a breath. 'Freitas, Gallagher and Montmorency will make the election with Freitas working on his complexion. I know he's cutting out fried bread. But Gallagher's got an advantage with his make-up case – his mother's an actress. Molyneux doesn't have the looks, but his backers are relying on his personality. A mistake, in my view. Challenor could make it, but is not serious enough about it, and Malmescott is going to fall at the last.'

'I say, Dynevor, how do you know all this?'

'I just take an interest. It's something I happen to be rather good at. I'm not doing anything about it. I am allowed to take an interest, I suppose?'

'Bicker, bicker, bicker,' Cavendish sighed. I looked at the windows around Hop Quad (we were in Hop Quad), and then at the flagstones. I decided I had a weapon against Dynevor when he was like this: I ignored him.

We left College by the main gate and walked down Longwall Street. I always felt ill-at-ease outside College, but the other two had determined to snap some tea at Mrs Todds. I clasped my hands firmly behind my back. The College walls were built as if to protect us from the world outside – town yobs these days, but insurrection in those days; civil warriors, religious maniacs, creditors. There was a sense of wandering into another country, going into the town. Times were changing. There was a supermarket in Salisbury. Yes, and quite recently, a car park on several stories. There were boys – they may have been our age – who had cropped their hair to the skull. There was no need to do that. It was a new and irritating way of wearing their hair. Why did they do that? We put our hands in our pockets and held up our faces.

'Now here we are at Mrs Todd's. Will you fellows allow me to sock you a plate or two of something agreeable?'

'By all means you may,' we said.

In no time we were ensconced in the corner table looking out over the busy High Street. Here and there among the townspeople, boys in tailcoats sauntered in twos and threes. 'Do you think,' I asked, 'that Salisbury men would be as obviously Salisbury men if we didn't wear our get-up?'

'Oh law bless you,' Mrs Todd said, hands full of plates which brimmed with fresh cut loaf, and butter, and strawberry jam, and scones, and toast, and thick slabs of fruitcake. 'You young gentlemen, we'd know you if you were mother naked and in another country.'

'Thank-you, Mrs Todd,' Cavendish flourished his handkerchief. 'May I trouble you to ask your girl to give the fire a poke on your way down?'

'I'll see to that myself, young sir.'

'Too kind of you, Mrs Todd.'

'God!' muttered Dynevor, as the worthy old soul busied herself with the fire, then the stairs.

'What's that, Dynevor?'

'I mean it's pretty sickening, isn't it? "Young sir." I mean really.'

'What's wrong with that?' I demanded. 'Dear old soul.'

'I mean, I might be the King of Cumbria, but what would she do if she met the Queen of England?'

'Queen Victoria was so unpopular when she first came to the throne she threatened to abdicate unless the press stopped being witty at her expense.' Cavendish dusted the crumbs from his fingers. 'And yet by the 1880s, a sort of national hysteria had surrounded her. Empire. Dead Albert, that sort of thing. When she addressed the Corps at Winchester the whole parade fainted. When she spoke to a prefect at Harrow, he exploded.'

'What? Blew up?'

'Nothing left of him at all. The excitement was too much. We weren't like that at Salisbury. We thought she was a sordid old bag.'

'*Did* we now? Extraordinary thing.'

'She came to College once. Only the Christian enthusiasts stayed to cheer. Most threw fruit at them from the leads. The prevailing view likened her to a haggis-faced sack of anthracite.'

'*Did* we? Extraordinary.' Cavendish might have been morally questionable but he had a remarkable fund of interesting information. I don't know why these things go together, but they always seem to. 'Being that as it may, Cavendish. The Smoker. How can we reliably fix it so that Dynevor fails miserably in the election?'

'May I just say,' Dynevor put in, 'it's perfectly all right to talk about me as if I weren't here.'

'Well, why shouldn't we?'

'No reason at all, I've just said so.'

'Then why mention it?'

'Oh knock it off you two,' Cavendish broke in. 'You're worse than my parents the way you go on. Tell me what acts the others are having a dash at.'

Dynevor ran through the list in extraordinary detail. Then he came to Fluke, at which Cavendish perked up. 'Fluke is registered as a Shakespearian monologue. I happen to know it is the Agincourt speech from *Henry V*.'

'I say,' I said, 'Fluke hasn't got much idea has he? Gentlemen of England now abed? Once more into the breach dear friends? That's not the ticket is it?'

'Oh I don't know,' Cavendish mopped his face, mop, mop, wipe, wipe. He was almost having one of his turns. 'So: Molyneux, Challoner and Turbot are going for an ambitious triple at, what? Eleven to eight?'

'Exactly.'

'Malmescott plays a clever game, bringing a Blood on stage with him. I'd put him at six to four on.'

'Even money,' Dynevor put in deftly.

'Really? Whose book?'

'Courtley's.'

'You *have* been getting around, young fellow,' I said admiringly.

'I take it I am allowed *that*? To get *around* is all right, isn't it?'

'Bickering, bickering,' Cavendish smoothed the turbid water. 'I think it is clear how Dynevor should proceed. We'll register him today on Courtley's book. We'll put him down for a Shakespearian monologue, and Carnahan will give the toothsome little unit some breathing space.'

I wished they wouldn't call Dynevor things like 'toothsome little unit'. I'd no idea what it meant, but I didn't like it. 'Which monologue?' I demanded.

Cavendish made a gesture: 'The Second Witch's speech from Macbeth. "Fair is foul, and foul is fair, hover through the fog and filthy air." '

'Brilliant! A masterstroke!'

'But foul *is* also fair, Wynn-Candy. We must remember

that Dynevor here in his stage make-up could recite a dictionary of infestive diseases and win by acclaim. Dynevor will have to look the part.'

'Witches would have very red lips,' Dynevor said excitedly, 'and luminously white faces, and their fingernails would be incarnadine.'

Cavendish fluttered his handkerchief in Dynevor's face. 'The witch you will be playing will be less well-favoured. Your witch will have suffered from extensive malnutrition when young, and a diet of worms thereafter. Warts shall flower on her face. She will be dressed in blood. She will speak like a dog.'

'Ha ha!' I cried, 'A masterstroke! *She* won't be courting popularity!'

'And afterwards,' Dynevor asked, 'Won't Carnahan hate me more than he does now?'

'No.'

'Why not?'

'Because he couldn't hate you any more than he does.'

It was perfect. Dynevor started to tell how he'd played Titania at prep school. I began to glow. Cavendish sat adjusting his tie. We were a contented trio over the piled-high plates of scones and toast, and Gentleman's Relish. You can see why they call them the happiest days, when Gentleman's Relish could make you happy.

Death by tarts

We went back immediately to register our contender at Trading Post. It was a sensation in College. 'Dynevor!' they said. 'The Toothsome Unit!' 'He's in the traps, The Succulent One!' A crowd began to gather and, in the excitement, Dynevor turned his eyes on. I didn't immediately stop him. As a result of that, word travelled like magic. The news left our end of College and appeared at the other without going through the space in between. That doesn't happen in England any more, now that we've done away with mutinies. Within six hours the total book had trebled, wagers coming in from as far away as a regimental mess in Mozambique.

It was a matter of moments before a huge face appeared round our door and laughed at us. It was Carnahan come to congratulate us. 'A cabal! I congratulate you! Ha ha! Wynn-Candy you fox! You've had a hand in this, don't deny it! Good man! It's a certainty! And yet, do you know? Do you?'

We said we didn't.

'That fathead at Courtley's gave me six to two on! What do you think of that!'

'You might lose your pound, of course, please Carnahan,' I said riskily.

'Wynn-Candy, you're a good sort, but you know very little about money. You think it's all ten-and-sixes.' He drew me confidentially aside. 'I'm going to win forty-five pounds!'

It was then that I realised we had made a terrible mistake. Carnahan had bet an inconceivable amount of money; money enough in those days to fund an invasion of a Middle Eastern protectorate. 'But how am I going to pay him back?' I cried in anguish. 'How? How? How?'

Cavendish looked exasperated. 'Pay back whom? Whom are you going to pay back?'

'All those poor saps who've laid out on Dynevor who we've put in to lose.'

'Enough's enough!' he cried, exasperated. I leapt to my feet. When you live at close quarters, in charged circumstances, you are never far from a fight. You have to defend yourself.

'Wynn-Candy listen to me.' We circled each other in the tiny cell. 'You are not . . . a social worker, Wynn-Candy.'

'Whatever a social worker is, no, I'm not,' I agreed.

'We are all of us on a course downwards, aren't we? *Aren't we*? My particular slippery slope, Wynn-Candy, lies among the crackling sheets of an extended bachelorhood. Yours in some water buffalo, no doubt. People will go to hell in their own individual way!'

'No! *I don't want to go to hell.*'

'You're in a minority! Keep your damn minor views about that to yourself. Let Dynevor do what he wants! You are deforming his personality! You are twisting him cruelly! You are destroying him! Leave him be: You are not your brother's keeper!'

'Yes I am.'

'Dynevor is not your brother! You will just get hurt!'

'I've already been hurt, I don't mind! I just don't want to go to hell!'

'Listen to me Wynn-Candy. I want to say something very serious to you.'

'Thank God! What is it?'

'You are thinking, Wynn-Candy. And you are not allowed to think. You have nineteen juniors, *and you are not allowed to think*.'

'But who will answer for it? Who will answer!' I wailed.

'What's the question?'

He had me there. I struggled a bit and gave up. 'When I have twenty juniors is this what I will think? Is this where thinking leads you?' I asked him. 'If it is, will I have to think? Or is it a privilege I can flag?'

I wandered off with my head in turmoil. Even the rag in Maldon ('I cry! I cry!' *two* fellows said) failed to lift my spirits. I changed into my togs and went out on to Little Acre where the posts stood up white against a sky of dishwater. Scattered boys in muddy colours moved about the puddles.

'Hello Hog,' I said.

'Hello Wynn-Candy.'

'What are you up to, then?'

'Oh I'm just mucking about.'

'Look here, Hog, you've got a crisp tackle on you. Why don't you show Dynevor how it's done?'

'David is a genius. I don't show a genius how to do anything.'

'Who's David?'

'It's what I call Dynevor.'

'Why do you call him that?'

'It's his name.'

'No it's not. His name is Dynevor. Never mind that. Look here, I don't mean to be rude or anything, but Dynevor, whom I have acquired, is as spoilt as all-get-out, and a bit touched, perhaps, but he is no genius.'

Hog span the ball in his hands, then he set it up. 'Can you kick this goal?' he asked.

'Well, Hog, let's see. From here . . .' We were facing College, ten yards from the half way, a forty yard kick with the wind coming across from behind. 'I could get one out of three.'

'How about *that way*?' Hog turned and pointed at the other goal posts.

'No. Sixty yards? Into the wind? Of course not, no.'

Hog span the ball. 'Dynevor is a genius,' he said.

'Are you saying Dynevor could kick that?'

'He's a genius for it.'

Sixty yards and the breeze freshening above the pitch – a crow beating into the wind. 'He'd never do it'.

'He'd keep it low until the last third. Then the spin he'd put in would lift it, and the ball would bite back into the wind and dig down to the goal. I've seen him do it. He's a genius.'

'Well, it beats me. Do you want to kick two-up till the others arrive?'

'If you'd like to Wynn-Candy.'

'I'll go behind the goalposts then.'

So Dynevor could kick could he? The tackle was beyond him. He couldn't face the flying heels; intimidated by the hips; and the knees that come up smartly under your chin if you don't dominate your man. But he could kick. He could do half the job. It was a shame – a damned shame – that it was the wrong half. College fullbacks were tacklers first and foremost. That gangling, fearless Buxton of the XV. He went for his man with eight foot arms going like a gaucho's bolas to wrap themselves several times round a man's lower legs. Not a particle of fear in him. Been concussed too many times to be afraid of anything.

But Dynevor was not a fullback. Never could be. Hadn't been concussed enough. Afraid of everything. But at least Carnahan was treating him in a more fraternal way. More like a brother. I say like a brother. Cain was somebody's brother, was he not? 'Come on, Diddums, tackle me now!' he'd shout, and he'd toddle past Dynevor as if his boots were laced together. 'Wackle me Wynevor!' And when Dynevor did he'd make a great fuss of rolling on his back, squeaking 'Hee hee hee!' with simulated terror.

'If Carnahan goes on like that, I'll kill him!' Dynevor stamped his foot in my cell. He was such a difficult child.

'Now what? You're complaining again. What are you complaining about now?'

'Carnahan is mocking me in practice.'

'You've got to learn to laugh at yourself, Dynevor! And just be grateful he's not trampling you into the turf any more.'

'He is making fun of me, and I hate him.'

'You're never satisfied, are you Dynevor? There's always something to complain about.'

'Well what else is there!' he cried wildly. 'You said people would treat me properly if I behaved properly. And they don't! And we never go out! And I'm not allowed to do any of the things I enjoy, you keep me cooped up here, I don't have any fun any more!'

'You like it when Cavendish chats to you.'

'*Chats* to me! *Cavendish*!'

'Look on the bright side, dear boy!'

'The bright side is that I'm going in front of the College Bloods with warts on my face to make a laughing stock of myself!'

'Look here Dynevor. You don't *want* to be a College Tart! Do you know what they do? Do you know what they actually *do*?'

'Of *course* I know. Of *course* I know what College Tarts *do*.'

'Then I'll tell you. Tarts just sit around all day long giggling and gossiping and passing notes to each other and giving them to College men.'

'Which is *exactly* what I'm best at!'

'And it is very bad for their characters. Remember this: an action forms a habit. A habit forms a character. A character forms a destiny.'

'Who told you that? Dr de Zoete?'

'He didn't actually.'

'I should think not. It sounds like one of those bits of wisdom you get in the *Reader's Digest*.'

'And what's wrong with that!' I demanded indignantly.

'Oh don't be so *stupid* Wynn-Candy! You are *so thick*!'

I must have reacted somehow to that because he apologised immediately. 'You are what you are. As I am what I am. If I am anything, anymore.' And he sighed, put his chin in his hands and looked out of the tiny window.

'I'm only trying to help.'

'I know! I know! I wish you'd stop! I can't tell you how I wish you'd *just leave me alone*!'

We were a sorry couple, as the mechanics of kindness closed in on us. Boys of my level didn't call to us because of Dynevor, and boys of his level didn't call to us because of me. He wouldn't speak because he didn't want to, and I didn't speak because I had nothing left to say. Imagine the picture of misery of which we were the foreground figures.

Where was the rat on the fishing line? The blowpipes? The bladder in Maldon Hall? We were awkward round the braziers and diffident in goal. And yet, however we dipped into the well of depression, life teemed around us. We had nine members of our Roof in the top three football teams; we had the Captain of Rackets; two of us were in the Small Choir; Delavera was a certainty for Elysium; Robertshaw was in the Colts, and when we said we had a Hog, College went Hurrah! He scored two tries against Harrow: at full stretch he'd dug his forward heel in five yards from the line, two tackles skidded on the turf in front of him – he dived over the line, hoop-la! Hog! Hog! Hog! If he'd done that twelve times more we would have won the match.

And indeed, looking back on the bright side, there was a personal moment too. I advanced in the Cadet Corps. The Sergeant Major told me: 'Now, Mr Wynn-Candy, your shooting has improved this term. I've got your scores here. I want to put you down for Bisley. Are you up to it?'

'Gosh I hope so, Sarn't Major.'

'God preserve you from being under fire, sir, but in competition shooting there is a worse thing: you've got no enemy to hate.'

'No enemy. Right Sarn't Major.'

'Except, there is one enemy.'

'There is, is there?'

'The hardest enemy to defeat there is.'

'Who's that, Sarn't Major?'

'You are.'

'I'm the enemy. Right Sarn't Major. I see.'

'You see a duck's arse in a Scotch mist, sir. But I've put you up for full corporal. I'm telling you this because I want you a sergeant for Bisley. Sergeants frighten the enemy.'

Which was me. I was to be made a sergeant to frighten myself into defeat. The Sergeant Major had been regular army till recently and his reasoning was beyond us. It may not have been logical, but logic had let me down that term already. I liked the Sergeant Major.

Dynevor said 'Corporal Wynn-Candy. Now you'll be able to boss everybody about. And if they disobey, you can shoot them.'

'You might take an interest at least.'

'All right, I'll try and take an interest. Are you going to stand to attention and all that sort of thing?' There was nothing to say to that. So he said 'That's about as much as I can be interested in the army, do you mind?' And then there was a scene.

In fact, let me hop ahead of several dreadful scenes. Shocking scenes. I hate scenes, so I've forgotten them. But there would have been a threat of suicide. People threatening suicide. You don't take that seriously, do you? I certainly didn't.

It was the devil of a job to get the little beast dressed for the Smoker. He muttered, and snapped, and pursed his lips, and broke into wild but muted cries as his wardrobe was laid out. 'I'm to appear in this sack, am I? And this is a mop for me? And this hat thing?'

'And the warts,' I reminded him.

'Not the warts! Oh please not the warts! Please don't make me wear warts!'

'Without warts,' Cavendish told him, 'You will triumph over your disadvantages. Warts are essential.'

'Now pull yourself together, dear boy,' I told him. 'And practise your speech again. How are you going to say it?'

'I think he should say it in a gulping sort of croak, like an epileptic,' Cavendish said. 'If epileptics do gulp. Do it like that, Dynevor, as if you're swallowing your tongue and about to suffocate.'

We couldn't make out what he was saying, so that didn't work. 'All right. Try it jeering, Dynevor, no-one likes that.'

'I don't know how to jeer,' he said coldly.

'Oh *don't* you?' Cavendish jeered at him.

'*No*, I *don't*' Dynevor jeered back. 'Oh I *see*, I'm awfully sorry. Now how did I do that? . . . *No*, I *don't*! . . . Let me see . . . Fair is foul and foul is fair . . .' he jeered.

'By George I think he's got it!' I cried.

'The voice is still intoxicating. It is a cherub's voice. It is the voice of a diminutive angel. It won't do for us. Tell me, Dynevor, have you ever been to Lancashire?'

So it was that the Smoker saw Dynevor coming on third in the run, dressed in sackcloth, splashed with warts, hair like hell, reciting the Second Witch's speech in a Mancunian cleaning woman's accent.

The Chief Tart, Daisy, played with his nails, rolled his eyes, cocked an eyebrow, banged his gavel and ordered Dynevor from the stage. The audience in a kindly moment ignored our friend. The back row linked arms and, anticipating the balcony scene from *Private Lives*, sang through his piece. 'Saaaarm day I'll find you, moonlight behind you.' Through the eye of bat and tongue of toad, the hall sang 'Troooo to the drrream I've been drrrreaming . . .' No-one saw him leave the stage.

Carnahan in the gallery rubbed his finger in the runnels of his huge fists. His deckquoit lips were compressed in a wedge of disapproval. He saw me, and called down 'Don't think your trick worked. I never trusted *you*, Winky! Not after you and your postal order!' He laughed 'Hee hee hee!' but not enthusiastically.

Cavendish looked at me in a strange way, a guilty way. 'Never mind Carnahan, I'll square his money off for you. I made an absolute packet on the betting.' He saw me change I suppose. I was very shocked by what he'd done. He then said 'The important thing is we've got him to ourselves now.'

'Who?' I said.

'Dynevor, of course,' he said. 'Eh?'

Got Dynevor to ourselves? 'Eh?' Cavendish repeated, 'Eh?' As I looked into his face, it was as though he had drawn open the curtains for a moment and let me look into his cellar. I stepped back from the cellar steps, I can tell you. I stepped back and left the Smoker there and then, and wandered distractedly through the backways. Cavendish had *bet* on the outcome, *knowing* we'd fixed Dynevor. Our little runner had done *that* (and at some cost to himself), and Cavendish had '*made a packet on it*'. People waved to me through the shadows and I waved back, but I had been horribly disillusioned by one who had been close for so long, a cellmate I had admired and trusted.

I found him swaying in our cell. Holding himself and rocking to and fro. 'I am completely wiped out,' he said in a dull voice. 'I've got no friends. No-one admires me. I don't know who I am any more.'

'You were heroic, Dynevor. A hero.'

'Yes,' he said, and smoothed his sack with the flat of his hand. 'I am no-one now. That's what you want, isn't it? All right. I will cease to exist. I shall be nothing.' He looked around vaguely. 'I didn't like the one they call Daisy, did you?'

That was when I thought he was going to be all right. 'Trample him on the football pitch!'

'No,' he said quietly, 'I won't do that.'

'Well, I should think you'd be relieved anyway. Now we can make a completely new start. We can make a respectable citizen out of you. Doesn't that make you glad?'

'I am not glad, I am dead.'

'You're not dead. You're just growing up.'

'Am I? Is that what growing up is like? Dying, and losing everything?'

Yes. As far as I knew. I was not the only one, surely, to have been aware of a clearing in a wood. I had not been alone, I think, watching a boy with the Beaker People round his neck. Hun gun dun. So I said 'I should think so.'

He looked around a bit. He fidgeted. He played with the inside of his lapel. 'I shall have to find something to do, I suppose.'

'Yes of course. How about small bore shooting?'

'If I can't be popular, perhaps I should be the opposite.'

Realising this was a prelude to a bout of introspection I said 'It's been a long day. We're probably both tired. You'll feel better after a good night's sleep.'

He said 'You have murdered sleep, Wynn-Candy.'

'Rot!'

'Oh *won't* you release me from the bargain now?'

'After all we've been through?' I asked him sadly.

'I've nothing left.'

'Nothing left to lose,' I told him, 'but everything to gain.'

He certainly had no position any more. Strangers would stop him and say '*You* think you're funny, but you're *not*.' He didn't like that. Nor when the College Tarts snubbed him horribly. He was like the Queen who never smiled again.

Then he got into trouble during prep – a fight in The Pit – and he was sent up to be beaten. Not to be seriously beaten as for failing one's Liberties, but a sort of congratulatory beating (fighting in prep was approved of), to have no more than the College arms imprinted on his person.

He walked up the Long Chamber to the Ushers' Dayroom and went inside. After a moment we heard the most appalling scream, like a circular saw biting into timber. '*Eeeeeeeeeeeeeeeeeeeaaaaaaaaaaarrrrrrrrrggggggghhh-hhhhhhhowwwwwwwww*!' And then there was silence. The door opened. The call went up: 'Faaag!' The last tug to the door was sent up to the San for the doctor.

That was the last we saw of him through that term. He was carried up to the San with a suspected seizure. Some sort of epilepsy. Some sort of fit sort of thing. It was a measure of his new status that it caused no comment. He went up for tests and nobody knew he was gone. Even I didn't miss him. That was odd, wasn't it? After all we'd been through?

His face had gone. The face of the Afghan girl I'd first seen glowing in a laundry skip. He'd taken his face off after the Jump Supper, and sticking to his end of the bargain, he'd never put it on again. Because he didn't have another face to wear he had walked around facelessly. That's why no-one knew whether he was there or not.

There was no medical verdict on him. He came out looking pale and inconclusive. they never tried to beat him again. The parliamentary whip had been withdrawn. He had rejected College discipline. So he disappeared.

Curiously though, he came out to our kickabouts now and then, and when Carnahan had the ball Dynevor would run up the touchline looking, with a sinister fixity, at Carnahan's legs. He was up to something, but no-one knew what.

My new best friend, Rowse, heard that he was planning to become the most hated boy in the history of the College.

'He won't manage it,' Cavendish said. 'No, no, no, he can't do that.' Cavendish and I, we were polite with each other, we shared the same cell, but things had changed between us. He'd betrayed many of his friends and all his colleagues in an act of cleverness. 'No, Dynevor won't pull that off. There's too much competition. He'll never be more hated than Carterton. He sent a telegram to Goering in 1940 offering to sell them the College for an administrative capital after Germany won the war.'

'There you go again with your nonsense.'

'It may be nonsense, but at least it's mine!' he cried. 'Why do you think that any nonsense should be yours! Why won't you let people be nonsensical on their own account! You've killed Dynevor! Killed him! And I helped you! I can't bear it! I can't bear it!' He turned his head into his hands and sobbed.

'I've no idea what you're talking about,' I said.

'Haven't you!' He slammed his fist impotently on his armchair. 'Haven't you? Have you never looked into his eyes, then?'

Into the eyes that had saved my life, with their lemon flecks, in the room, on somebody's lap . . . 'Certainly not,' I said. 'And as for the nonsense you talk . . . you might as well talk it, if you want. I don't mind any more. I've given up.'

Cavendish blew his nose and looked up at me. I was afraid he'd draw his curtains back again so I said, 'Your move.'

'Is it? Checkmate. Fancy another?'

Dynevor victorious. We don't like that

The winds of change had begun to blow about our ribs. Didn't feel a thing. There you have the one disadvantage of being properly buttoned up: you can't feel a warning draught. But then I wouldn't have caught the warning anyway. The first thing that got blown away was the old way of playing football. And in the matter of football (don't laugh) I was a modernist.

Rugby football was the direct descendant of the Half Quad Game. A little known fact. For the first five hundred years of its life football had been a fast, free-ranging game covering several parishes. Teams of two or three hundred men on each side. There was passing, and trampling, kicking one another between the posts – in fact many hallmarks of the game as it's played today by the All Blacks. The difference was that medieval football had many fatalities and no rules to speak of. You've seen Gaelic Football? Exactly.

However, in the middle of the nineteenth century, a Foundation Scholar got carried away with the exertions of the traditional game, running around a two hundred square mile pitch; he fell on the ball, called in his colleagues to fall on top of him, and they held the ball until the whistle went, just before Christmas. This style of play became popular, for both social and financial reasons. Small economies would spring up in these proto-mauls (making book, establishing a trade in curious photographs) and primitive fortunes would be made and lost over the course of a three-day game. The ball came to move only a few feet in an afternoon – and that downward.

This game became more convenient, and cleaner, to play in College itself. Thus the Half Quad Game.

Then a strange splinter group of medievalists took the Half Quad Game out of Half Quad sometime in the middle of the nineteenth century. Perhaps they were unpopular, perhaps they were anxious for some exercise. Perhaps it was mere affectation. But they took a bladder out onto the meadows away from College and played the Half Quad Game in the mud. It was known (by us at least) as Salisbury football. Why it was known by others as Rugby football is down to the ruthless and rather insane ambitions of Dr Arnold. We won't go into that.

A century later, in my first year, football remained a horizontal, scrum-locked game. Why it started to move none of us knew. There were changes in the rules perhaps (the lower classes buying washing machines on credit comes to mind again) but whether that was the bottom of it I can't say. But in one year the amount of running went up like this, and the communal life in sporting slums went down like that.

This made the game ever more popular in College, even though other schools had one hundred years more experience in running around with the ball.

We could give one another a game though, and we played Cock House every year amongst ourselves. Our Roof had done well that year. We were in the final for the first time. By no means the favourites we had scraped through partly through luck (a *lot* of food poisoning) and partly through sheer, simple, singleminded determination (we'd bored Bewley's into submission).

I, unfortunately, was not playing. Carnahan had broken three of my ribs in tackle practice. Normally this wouldn't have mattered but the wheezing noise in my chest made them suspect a punctured lung, and on the Chaplain's advice (he doubted my soul was in a fit state to risk a transition) I scratched from the team. We expected to lose for reasons other than that. Our opponents had all the backs of the College XV, and the XV hooker to ensure possession, and the tallest boy in the county (he never jumped in the lineouts because he never had to). We didn't expect to win. We were happy to lose bravely. That was what we were good at.

'Freaks,' Cavendish said on the sideline (he was a satirist). 'Look at that little hooker with those vile little legs.' He looked yearningly at Dynevor who had, for reasons of his own, joined us. Cavendish made a face at me, but I avoided it. 'And that beast on stilts in the lineout. Ugh!' He looked at Dynevor again. Nothing. What was Dynevor *doing* here?

'Roof! Roof! Roof!' I yelled. I was yelling 'Roof!' because we were playing Mowbray's which wasn't a Roof, it was only a House. I thought this might rattle their confidence. The thought was wrong, but without twenty juniors I wasn't surprised.

From the first whistle our scrum put on a show of dumb resistance against the opposition. Mowbray's had a confusing way of running at us, and passing the ball among themselves. We'd tackle one, and he'd pass to another of his team before he fell. This may not have mattered, but our fellows played with such grit and commitment that three of our chaps would take each ball-carrier by the ankles. After five such tackles all our side would be on the ground, and twelve of the opposition would trot across a fallen field to have a party under our goalposts.

I didn't like that.

It wasn't cheating exactly, but I didn't like it. They'd worked out some secret formula for winning. That's not very sportsmanlike, is it?

But don't misunderstand. We didn't give a fig whether we were to win or lose. Both sides were to win or lose as well as they possibly could. That was how we played the game.

'Roof! Roof! Roof!'

We had taken possession of a fumbled pass. The ball was collared by Fortescue who slung it back to Carnahan who was foaming at the mouth. Carnahan raced off the mark with Delavera on the outside. Five three-quarters converged on Carnahan but he was going to trample them: he went straight at them; set his chest at them.

Then something happened which took our breath away. Delavera had looped round outside Carnahan, running watchfully beside him, hands cocked for the pass that never came. Then suddenly he broke inside, moving at speed behind him. He emerged on the blind side – and this was magic you wouldn't see at the Palladium – with the ball in his hands! The five three-quarters fell over backwards trying to change direction. Delavera's body lifted off the pitch as the wind filled his sails. A fullback came for him, the fearless Buxton, arms like the fighting tentacles of a squid snaking out for their prey. Delavera grubbed the ball with the inside of his foot right under Buxton's face, and he sailed past untouchable. The ball kicked up into the pit of his stomach, and he scored under the posts, swinging his hair out of his eyes.

'Oh well done Roof!' our opponents cried.

We immediately subdued our spirits. 'Pure fluke. Frightfully bad luck on Buxton, he so nearly got him.'

You watch your losing team score and you keep your composure because you don't dare assume you'll win (do you watch England play much?) We scored another four times up to half time using the same trick. You see how the spirits of a match swing from one team to another. We were suddenly playing with a wild confidence, we played with a reckless spontaneity, we were playing like Tongans and Mowbray's was utterly confused by it. Marvellous to watch. It wasn't as if we'd *planned* to do it, it just happened.

Then the spirit swung away from us and no-one scored all through the second half, battle as the Titans might. The tackling was desperate, the scrimmaging ferocious. We'd got the hang of them in the scrum – only two of us tackled one of them now *and we got up quickly afterwards*. But they'd got the measure of Delavera in the centre, and they were coming in cunningly to smother the reverse pass. So we went up and down the pitch till the two teams agreed to fall on the ball between the twenty-fives to get their breath back.

We were five points behind. The whistle was due. Carnahan had a seizure. He ripped the ball out of a ruck (a hand still attached to it) and wheeled into space throwing midgets off his body. He trampled two, he leapt over three, he went down with a roar, flinging the ball to Hog. Hog span it across two men in the line to Delavera. Delavera beat a tackle and worked forward first with a hand-off (*down* he went into the mud), and then with a sidestep (*over* he went with his boots in the air). Then, sensing the imminent whistle he aimed a long, low kick right down the pitch, and Carnahan came chasing.

Buxton was there. Buxton had it covered with his tentacular arms as the ball came tumbling towards him, skittering end over end. The rugby ball is an awkward shape, perhaps for this reason, and a yard from his hands the point of the ball dug into the pitch and flipped up over his head. Carnahan roared round Buxton's flailing grip and one-handedly gathered the ball a foot from going out; he buried his head in his chest and came down touch from the ten-yard line with a clear run to the goal. The shouts of the crowd were deafening, overwhelming, like the thunder of blood in the ears of God. Don't quibble. You weren't there. That is *exactly* what the shouts of the crowd were like, and they lifted us into an ecstasy of excitement.

Then the following things happened in quick succession. Dynevor threw off his dufflecoat. He raced on to the pitch. He ran low and fast, he went like an arrow, and flung himself at Carnahan's pounding legs. He caught him expertly at the knees, he scooped them together, he knocked them waist-high, he brought Carnahan down in the finest crash tackle ever seen on Big Side. Carnahan went through 180 degrees, his head drove into the ground, causing a hairline fracture of the spine. Then the whistle went. The game was over.

How could a boy such as I was then make clear his feelings? When the stretchers came on to take Carnahan and Dynevor away (neither moved)? When the referee awarded us a penalty try? When the conversion under the posts failed. When Mowbray's clapped us off the pitch with many expressions of condolence?

We wandered distractedly in twos and threes from the field of play. I remember there were birds in the sky again, wheeling in the failing light. We said nothing to one another, but I knew what I had to do. I steeled myself. Dynevor had gone too far. He had gone beyond the jurisdiction of normal human experience.

My steps led me past Martyr's Memorial and I stood there a moment passing my hand across my temple. This was a site of great pain and sacrifice. I turned and went into the San.

He lay on his pillows. His colour was back. He had his face again. 'Dynevor,' I said to him.

'Hello, Wynn-Candy,' he said. 'Do you think I've done well? Do you think I'll be as hated as you hoped? Have I done well after all?'

'Dynevor,' I said to him.

'I'd been planning it for ages, you know. To make you proud of me, as you wanted.'

'Dynevor,' I said.

'I've done so much what you wanted, Wynn-Candy, but you see, it is not in me to be a respectable person.'

'Dynevor,' I said.

'But I've kept your bargain so long, and it has been so hard, and now I think you should release me, Wynn-Candy.'

'Dynevor,' I said, 'I've come to tell you something. What I have come to tell you is this. After what you have done today I realise that I must release you from our bargain. It has not worked out. You must follow your nature, and I must follow mine.'

'Thank-you, Wynn-Candy.' He leaned back with a contented smile.

'I have no authority over you any more, and therefore I have no responsibility. This is goodbye.'

'No, no, no Wynn-Candy. You haven't got that right at all. You can release me from my side of the bargain. But I'm not going to release *you*. You promised you'd look after me. And now you have saved my life. Now you must always look after me.'

I turned away sadly, shaking my head at him. He didn't seem to care at all. Would he never learn?

'Wynn-Candy?'

I turned. 'Yes?' I could not see him.

He said gently 'I won't come to you for anything until I am cheered in College.'

'You never will be. You don't exist any more. I will never never see you again.' The room was swimming. I never could do goodbyes. I would never see him again, and he didn't care at all.

'You think everyone hates me, and despises me, and scorns and ignores me, don't you?'

I shrugged at the ceiling.

'Do you know how long that will last?'

I shrugged at the window.

He snapped his fingers weakly. 'Pop! That long.' He snapped them again, decisively. 'Pop!'

I walked out. As I closed the door and walked away I heard him calling softly after me: it was like a sort of song, like mermaids. 'I'm not releasing you Wynn-Candy. You've taught me that at least!'

Intermezzo

After that gruelling Michaelmas half, Hilary followed, and Trinity followed that. The summers, I assume, were particularly glorious. The sun was always shining then, we burnt like berries. And there would have been the click of bats, and shadows in the long grass. Bracken fields. Elms twinkling in the distance. I affected a hat I remember, and sat in a tree with it. How we ached in class for the bells which released us into the water meadows to run with our books, and hampers, and screwtop bottles, and fishing lines, each to his own. Dressed in loose whites from cricket, in pressed flannels we cycled up to Equerries in gangs of good fellowship.

Rowse and I went off by ourselves that summer. We'd stroll down to lie by the crook of the river, in the roots of Lufton's Elm, looking down into the deep pool, scouting for the pike that was reputed to live there. I never saw the pike, but there was a kingfisher, there were water rats, there were fish rising for mayflies in the evening, making circles in the stream.

Strange things happen to you when you look at lazy water, without a thought in your head. You become very quiet, and deep, and time slides through you without adding to your age.

Once, hidden there, concealed in the roots and intent on the water, we heard childish voices. With irritation we heard them because the pike was a cunning fellow, he was cautious. That was why he was two hundred years old. He wouldn't come up with that racket going on. I raised a head above the root to see.

Five tugs, Cavendish, and Dynevor spread out towels, and stripped off on the river bank. They lay down in the sun in that secluded spot, protected by bushes and a screen of trees. Then, led by Dynevor, they started to do something that sickened me. They must have thought they were unobserved. They weren't afraid of observers as they indulged themselves. I hated it like poison. That sort of vice can get into a school and infect it. And once it is in a school it is hard – damned hard – to get it out again. And, you know, it isn't just the vice itself, it's the knock-on effect. All sorts of College activities suffer. The standard of sport goes down, for one. And boys have their minds on the vice when they should be concentrating on better things. Looking for a pike, for instance.

I resolved to put a stop to it there and then. I stood up and said 'I know what you're doing and you will stop it *right* this instant! That filthy habit will stop *right now*.'

Their hands flew behind their backs in a guilty manner. 'Cavendish, I'm disappointed in you.'

'Oh it's all right, it's only Wynn-Candy,' Cavendish said, and calm as you please, laughing even, they fell back to their vile practice. I jumped off the elm root and waved an ashplant at the nearest offender. I snatched the offending thing out of his mouth and said 'Don't you realise what you're doing to yourself like this?'

'It's only a smoke, Wynn-Candy,' he said insolently.

'It's not only a smoke, you little fool!' And I told him what effect the evil little things had on a sportsman's wind. Dynevor laughed and stood provocatively at the water's edge, holding his cigarette between his teeth. I shoved him in the chest and he went into the water. He fell, with comic exaggeration, on his back, but kept his cigarette dry. He floated in the deep water puffing ostentatiously and laughing 'Cool as a mountain stream!'

When I told him about Gammer Gurton, he didn't believe me ('Pikey, pikey, pikey!'). But he slowed in his mockery when I explained the reason for the beast's peculiar name (teeth like needles). His composure disappeared and he paddled as inconspicuously to the bank as he could. 'I said I'd never ask you for anything until College cheered me, Wynn-Candy,' he said, 'So I'm asking you now: pull me up please.' I wouldn't. Not until he foreswore cigarettes would I pull him up the sheer three foot bank to safety.

'I *can't* promise,' he whined, 'I'm an *addict*. You can't ask addicts for promises! They don't work.' For a frightened boy he was a remarkable negotiator. My eyes drifted to a point beneath him and breathed 'Good Lord! Here he comes!'

'*I promise! I promise!*' And I popped him out like a cork.

'I told you I was an addict,' he said as soon as he was dry. 'You can't trust us to keep promises. So sorry.'

'Fair enough,' I said airily, but I was seething inside. 'But if I ever hear of you smoking cigarettes again, I'll haul you down by the hair and pitch you into the pool at night! Are you with me?' He didn't say anything. But I never heard of any of them smoking again. We never had a vice problem in our house.

However, you may have observed that Dynevor claimed to have been cheered by College. An obvious lie to an outsider, the extraordinary fact was – it was true. College had cheered him to the rafters. In just two short halves after the Cock House calamity, College had forgotten his past. Say what you like, public schools are forgiving institutions.

Left to his own nature, Dynevor had done well in Hilary. A short, sharp half of scouring winds and bleak skies. There were rumours about him. Because we didn't speak to him in the Long Chamber we didn't know how true they were. He had gone out into College to make his life. He was seen promiscuously with this one, and that one, then with the other. He made a speech at the Literary Society. He was asked to join the Choir. He fenced for the Junior Colts. The College Tarts once caught him and had him blackened by their men. 'Practising without a licence' they said. He declined to join the confirmation classes. We knew very little about him, and wanted to know less.

Then in the Trinity half he had a part in the play. In fact he had two parts, and he was cheered by College. It was the most remarkable rehabilitation since Martin Luther was canonised. Oh wasn't he? The point holds.

The play, by a dramatic irony, was *Macbeth.* I was First Murderer. Carnahan was Macbeth. Daisy was Lady Macbeth. Dynevor (late to audition) got Second Witch.

No-one knew Carnahan could act, but then he had that face, and there was his manner. In fact he didn't have to act at all, he did very well indeed.

'I think he'll do very well as my Macbeth,' Daisy said prettily to his entourage of tarts. He fluttered himself with a fan. 'Ah, Dynevor, isn't it? Second Witch. You won't have much work learning your lines at least.'

'I think you'll find there's more to acting than learning lines, Dusty,' Dynevor replied.

'Then you should have learned my name is not *Dusty*, you little *actor.*' Grown men quailed under that look.

'Er . . . Dynevor's not a tart you see, er, Daisy, what's-your-name,' I put in. 'He's not interested in things like that.' Can't stand bullying, you see. No need for it, Daisy shot me a look of spun poison and flounced away.

'Thanks, Wynn-Candy,' Dynevor said. It was the first time we'd spoken since Michaelmas in the San.

'Jolly bad luck you landing that particular part.'

'I said I'd do for Daisy, do you remember? Shall I tell you something funny? He can't act! Nobody's spotted it yet. Funny or not?'

I didn't like to tell the poor little sprat that it didn't matter whether the Senior College Tart could act or not. He was easy on the eye. That was the point. The Senior College Tart always took the female lead in the Trinity play. Mind you, the play was usually *Private Lives*, and there were certain points of difference between Amanda with her sweet voice and cocktail frocks, and Lady Macbeth. Particularly when playing opposite a College fullback carrying a twenty-two pound claymore, dressed in a suit of eight-inch nails. It was a very different fish. Carnahan had put in a request to play the part soused in blood – you didn't get that in Noel Coward. During rehearsals Carnahan told us 'I'm just going to sweat for a bit, but you tugs make believe it's blood, okay?' Very frightening man. He broke his own nose before the first night, deliberately or not I don't know. He practised his speeches to himself as he walked across the quads ('Is this a dagger I see before me?') with strange gestures. Not entirely gentlemanly, but frighteningly *committed.*

Daisy, on the other hand, giggled with his coterie in the 'green room'. On stage he hummed 'Some day I'll find you, moonlight behind you' when others were rehearsing. Almost, but not wholly inaudibly, the tarts would join in 'Trrrrrrrroo to the dream I am drrrrrreaming . . .' Maddening – in quite the wrong way – when you're working yourself up to a murder.

Carnahan caught them at it only once, and it was Daisy's undoing. Carnahan bore down on him with all the presence of a great ape. 'You, you're an *evil* piece of work, aren't you? You're a *vicious* little baggage aren't you? You're a cruel, jumped-up little sow, aren't you, Lady Macbeth?'

Daisy's expression said 'I'm not used to being spoken to like this,' but he kept silent. You would, when Carnahan was sweating, and we all knew it was blood coming out, and the big face was jammed up close, and the nails were touching you, and you were backed up against a pillar.

'But when you say "What? In our house?" you sound as though someone's farted at your birthday party. And that makes Macbeth look like a pansy. And *I am not a pansy*! You follow?'

Lady Macbeth collected herself as far as she could. 'How would you say it, then?'

Before Carnahan could speak, a voice all freighted with horror and guilt and fear came from the back of the stage. 'What? In our house?'

'*Exactly* like *that*!' Carnahan roared in Daisy's face.

'Oh that's a little serious, don't you think?'

Seeing the expression on Carnahan's armour, and fearing that Lady Macbeth would be torn to pieces, the director stopped the rehearsal. 'Macbeth, come and talk to me.'

Daisy collected her skirts, sought out the voice and faced it. 'Don't you know what's good for you, little actor?'

Dynevor said 'Well, I was standing at the back trying to understand a really evil piece of work, you see Dusty. Trying to feel how a *vicious* little baggage would speak, how a jumped-up little sow would do it, and I was surprised you hadn't got the hang of it.'

'You'll be sorry you started this, little actor. I'll have you off this play.'

What happened was this. The director cleared the set, holding back only the Macbeths and the witches. Then he gave Dynevor a Lady Macbeth speech to read. Carnahan nodded the great hairy coconut of his head twice in approval.

Dynevor took the book and his face became strange. His voice darkened. His eyes began to glow. Oh he was dangerously impressive. He frightened us. You could hardly watch if you had any religious convictions at all, the performance was an act of blasphemy.

'Well I can do *that*, obviously,' Daisy said. 'If you'd asked, I could have done *that*.'

'Good,' Carnahan said, 'Do it then.'

'What? Now? I'll need some time, surely, to rehearse.'

'This *is* a rehearsal,' the director said, suddenly bullish. 'Kindly do it, as Carnahan says.'

Daisy went reluctantly to the stage. He started the speech, and then he finished it. After what we had seen it couldn't have been worse if he'd been holding a tennis racket. Couldn't have been worse if he'd had a colander on his head. The director, one Mr Miller, knitted his fingers in a complicated and possibly painful way, and asked Daisy to do a Second Witch.

'Fair is foul, and—' Daisy began.

'Explore the sense of evil in the Second Witch.'

'Fair is foul, and—'

'Bring it back into the room here.'

'Fair is foul and—'

'Wait a second. I want you to try something that has just been suggested to me,' Mr Miller interrupted again.

Dynevor had insinuated his person onto the bench next to him. 'Give us a Second Witch with *strangeness*. Try the same piece with, ah, I don't know, a Lancastrian metal-worker's accent. Can you do that?'

'I haven't the faintest idea what a metalworker's accent sounds like.'

'Oh come now. Where does your family come from?'

'Cumbria, actually.'

'Then do it in a Cumbrian accent.'

'I was doing it in a Cumbrian accent. That's what we talk like in Cumbria.'

'That's how *you* speak in Cumbria.'

'That's how everybody speaks in Cumbria.'

'Even the taxi drivers? You surprise me.'

'No, the taxi drivers say, "A'y'up to th'yall then, are y'?" '

'Exactly. Do the speech in that voice.'

'But this isn't Cumbria. It's Shakespeare.'

'Look, when you're a director you'll know what is Cumbria and what is Shakespeare. Do it.' And he did. 'Interesting,' Mr Miller said.

'Very interesting,' Carnahan agreed.

'Second Witch? What do you say?'

Dynevor examined his nails. 'One of the many reasons you wouldn't want to be king of Cumbria.' When he caught up with me he said, 'Guess what Daisy's doing now? Second Witch.'

'Oh my dear fellow, I *am* sorry. That was your part. He is a vile, unscrupulous little oik!'

'Now ask who is Lady Macbeth?'

'Is it a riddle? Who is Lady Macbeth?'

'I am.'

'Oh I see! Do you mean to tell me that the Senior College Tart has gone to Second Witch, and you've taken his place? How on Earth did that happen?'

'Carnahan told them to do it.'

'Carnahan! But you tackled him unfairly and robbed us of Cock House!'

'Years ago.' Seeing my bafflement he dropped his face

for a moment and looked at me. 'There's been a lot of water under the bridge since then,' he said.

'Never mind that. You put Daisy through your Smoker piece. That was vindictive, don't you think?'

'But didn't you laugh?'

'No. You are ruthless Dynevor. You are cruel as well. These are not attractive characteristics. They are not worthy of a gentleman.'

'No. But they are useful to a gentleman.'

'I've been no good to you at all, have I?' I asked him sadly. 'I've taught you nothing at all.'

Indeed I hadn't. Far from satisfied with his campaign he put it to Mr Miller that the actor playing Lady Macbeth should be the same as that playing Second Witch. 'To elaborate the emotional resonances of the relationships.' He got Daisy pitched ignominiously off the play. He had no appetite for a limited victory. It was his character flaw.

At the end of term, his Second Witch wore a luminous white face, and incarnadine lips, and feral red nails. His Lady Macbeth was spellbinding. When he appeared on stage he gave off something that filled the senses of the audience with infinitely dangerous possibilities. His scenes with Macbeth caused College to breathe heavily, and sometimes to moan audibly.

But what made us roar and stamp our feet and cheer him to the rafters was his eyes. He turned his eyes on again. They gave out his substance into the audience. He allowed us to see through his eyes who he really was. That is something a gentleman hides from others. If he shows it, it is to one person in his whole life. Or at least to one person at a time. He does not distribute it wholesale, as through a firehose, to a dark hall full of strangers.

And so I lost him again. It was his nature to give himself to large numbers. He had the kicking ability to get him into a College team, and yet he preferred to stand conspicuous in the limelight. But still we clapped, and cheered, and stamped our feet. Delavera's face ran with visible tears. Cavendish mopped his face and blew his nose. College roared. Dynevor had found his place. There was a place for everyone at Salisbury College, no matter how eccentric, or indeed how doubtful.

That is the value of a public school education.

The evil elephant

'There is an evil elephant come into the school. Nobody saw it
come in. It came in bit by bit. But we must stamp it out and
destroy it!'

It should have been the happiest of times, but it was taken from me. In the very moment of victory the happiest days were cut short. Never known such days. For a schoolboy, the luxury and the liberty of his third year are irreplaceable. They are also indescribable. But why not try?

The study I'd been assigned was a tall hexagonal Tudor room with a small bay window and a window seat. It overlooked a secret quadrangle which had its own ravens. The Captain of Chant had a room on the other side, and he sang in the evenings. There was an old bell which struck three times every day. I had a fire, and a fender, and a small brocade-covered chair. I did not lack for company. A bird lived in the ivy outside my sill. There was a vagrant mouse. There were several earwigs and a school of silverfish. And dammit, I don't know why, there were Hog Robertshaw and Dynevor as well. I didn't want them, but they didn't want their basement room with the barrel vaulting, so they moved in with me.

'We don't like our cellar, so we've decided to move in with you,' Dynevor said. 'You don't mind, do you?'

'If you don't like it, my old turkey,' Hog said (he'd changed), 'you'll just have to lump it.'

'Oh *shall* I though?'

'Well what else will you do?'

'This is *my* study!'

'Make me some toast!' Dynevor waved his fingers at me.

'This is *my* study, *my* room, assigned to *me* not you. You're not senior enough, you're not *old* enough, you haven't *been* here long enough, and I *have*, so *stand up* when you listen to me! I can have you thrown out of here any time I choose!'

'Go on then.'

'Yes, go on.'

'Go on, have us thrown out.'

'Who'll he get to throw us out?'

'He obviously couldn't throw us out himself.'

I reared up at that, 'Well obviously I could, actually, for your information, I could throw you out like *that*!' I bit my thumb in their direction.

Dynevor turned away abruptly. He dropped his teasing tone. 'I say, I wish you hadn't done that.'

'Done what?'

'Bitten your thumb like that.' Dynevor looked at the back of his hands and spoke in a low voice. 'Where I come from that's like saying the worst thing you can about someone's mother. If we really had offended you, I'm sorry. You had only to ask us to leave and we would have gone.'

After a brief pause Robertshaw got up. 'Let's go,' he said crisply. He looked at me. 'I'm sorry, we've obviously offended you a great deal. I hope time can heal wounds that words obviously can't.'

'What the dickens are you talking about? I didn't mean to insult anyone's mother! For pity's sake stay and have some toast!'

'You're very kind, but it would be rude to my mother.'

'Oh come *on*! Grow up! Have some toast for heaven's sake!'

Dynevor sighed, and looked at the side of his hands. 'Have you got any Gentleman's Relish?' he asked. 'I can't eat toast without Gentleman's Relish. Have you got any?'

I hadn't, so I went and got some, and when I got back they'd moved in.

You wonder why I put up with them. I certainly wondered. Dynevor had come to put an energy and discipline into original ways of annoying you. For instance:

— he would sit for an hour over a sketchpad making lines and putting in the light and shade of a portrait. You'd try not to move too much. After an hour you'd go over and look at it and say 'That's not me!'

'Oh I don't know. The head has something.'

'Dynevor, I don't have four legs. I don't have a tail. You've been studying me for an hour and you've drawn a donkey!'

'I look beyond the outward show. I draw the essence.'

Then I wouldn't speak to him except to say 'Not funny. Not clever. Merely childish. Simply puerile. *Turn the damn light on Dynevor*! When the *hell* are you going to grow up?'

He'd turn the light off. I'd struggle over to turn it on. I'd turn and see him standing completely naked on a chair. He'd strip himself in twelve seconds. 'I am tree! I am bamboo!' He did it more than once. I never saw the funny side.

— they had a private language, one that no-one could understand. The thing about the language was that they couldn't understand it either. They made it up as they went along. There was only one linguistic rule in this system of non-communication. You could only use one word at a time. The word was 'Frobish'. Then 'Frobishtortlement'. The words became longer as the half developed. Then they became longer and longer. It became ridiculous. It became unrealistic. Unrealistic. One would say 'Frobishtortlementochkwatgrasskiterfric-
kenhollobotebensheballidrabumondebardlebattlebunke-
rlebardlefrequerdunderbumderstuntdermoindewatnotg-
roblerbobblegunterhockwatgrasskiterfrickenhollobount-
dermoindewatnotgrobblerbobblegunterhockwatgrasskit-
erfrickenholloboddertikanaweirobishtortlementuermoin-
dewatnotgrobblerbobblenterhockwatgrasskiterfrickenh-
ollobotebensheballikendodettlekrumdrabumondebardle-

battlebukerlebardlefrequerdunderbumderstuntdermoin-
dewatllnotgrobblerbobblegunterhockwatgrasskiterfrick-
enhollobotdermoindewatnotgrobblerbobblegunterhock-
watgrasskiterfrickenhollobodderg roddertikanaweirobis-
htortleatnotgrobblerbobblegunterhockwatgrasskiterfric-
kenhollobotebensheballikendodettlekrumdrabumondeb-
ardlebattlebunkerlebardlefrequerdunderbumderstuntd-
ermatnotgrobblerbobblegunterhockwatgrasskitenhollo-
bountdermoindewatnotgrobblerbobblegunterhockwatg-
rasskiterfrickenhollobodderg roddertikanaweirobishtortl-
ementtuntdermoindewatnotgrobblerbobblegunterhock-
watgrasskiterfrickenhollobotebenshebalikendodettlekru-
mdraondebardlebattlebunkerlebardlefrequerdunderbu-
mderstuntdermoindewatnotgrobblerbobblegunterhock-
watgrasskitefrickenhollobountdermoindewatnotgrobble-
rbobblegunterhockwatgrasskiterfrinotgrobblerbobblegu-
nterhockwatgrasskiterfrickenholonkerlebardlefrequerdu-
nderbumderstuntdermoindewatnotgroderstuntdfricken-
hollobotdermoindewatnotgrobblerbobblegunterhockwa-
tgrasskiterfrickenhollobodderg roddertikanaanaweirobis-
htortleatnotgrobblerbobblegunterhockwatgrasskiterfric-
kenhollobotebensheballikendodettlekrumdrabumondeb-
ardlebattlebunkerlebardlefrequerdunderbumderstuntd-
ermatnotgrobblerbobblegunterhockwatgrasskitenhollo-
bourickenhollobountdermoindewatnotgrobblerbobbleg-
unterhockwatgrasskiterfrinotgrobblerbobblegunterhock-
watgrasskiterfrickenhollonkerlebardlefrequerdunderbu-
mderstuntdermoindewatnotgrockenhollobodderg rodde-
rtikanawei?' one would ask.

And the other one would say 'Not without a *very* great deal of forethought.'

— and then they had deliberately irritating conversations:

Dynevor:	Precocibosity!
Robertshaw:	Plink!
Dynevor:	(thoughtfully) Beeeedardlearp?
Robertshaw:	(decisively) Dip.
Dynevor:	Dup?

Robertshaw: Biddle-up.
Dynevor: Biddleardleardleup!
Robertshaw: (scandalised) Ardlearrrrrp?
Dynevor: Arp.

More infuriating than it sounds. You'd be kneeling in Chapel to attend to your soul and there they were. 'Beedleop,' one saying. 'Debobble-op,' the other returning. You sat at Lufton's Elm looking for the pike in the deep pool and the silence would be broken by their whispering.

Dynevor: (archly) DebobblebumCandy.
Robertshaw: (significantly) Ardlearp.

Juvenile, you see. Puerile.

— they had a way of looking at what I was writing and making jokes about it to each other. I covered my work with my arm, and they silently climbed onto the cupboard top during prep and read what I'd written through a pair of binoculars. They repeated it to each other and shrieked with laughter. I said 'What the devil's so funny about that?' And they said, 'Barble?' and 'Dobble-op!'

Now in spite of this flamboyant infantilism, the two of them enjoyed a privileged status. Hog was the youngest member of the XXX, and Dynevor, while not officially a College Tart, was by acclaim the most glamorous tug in our community. He played in kickabouts and no-one was allowed to tackle him. They had both found their position – Salisbury was, as we've seen already, a strangely accommodating place.

It was, all told, a charmed existence, and we would all have been blessed had it not been for Dr Kennedy and our new Housemaster Mr Beesely. Dr de Zoete had died. Or had he gone to live in Cleveland? Or perhaps he'd had a stroke, it was a long time ago.

In the normal course of events a Housemaster was irrelevant; a remote ceremonial figure, like a soldier on a podium. He wasn't even allowed into the Long Chamber unless invited, he wasn't shirkable, so low was his status.

He was there in an advisory capacity, at least until he'd earned his Liberties.

So the fact of a new Housemaster would not be worth mentioning, but the winds of change were picking up into a stiff breeze.

He was a tubby man with an undistinguished face and tightly controlled hair rippling over his skull. His other characteristics were these: he had achieved rank in the Territorial Army, and he tried to match the spring in the Sergeant Major's salute:

BoyOyoOyoynngggggggg

(No-one could match the Sergeant Major's salute.)

And he couldn't run. You will want to see Mr Beesely running. That will tell you everything you need to know about him. Mr Beesely cantered tubbily in an upright stance, his chest out, and his head set back behind his shoulders. As his feet hit the ground in syncopated rhythm (buddum, buddum) they jarred his spine. *He held his elbows behind him.* When refereeing, as we see him now, he was at his most ridiculous.

The first game – as we remember – was used to drill the young tugs. Huntaway! The ball was booted way off across the pitch. The tugs on scrum-service went toiling after it, Beesely blew up for a penalty, and the tugs came toiling back again. The reason for the penalty? Dynevor wasn't putting enough effort into the game. 'Dynevor! Free kick against Dynevor for not putting enough effort into the game!' We were, as you may imagine, confused.

'Excuse me,' Dynevor said, 'I don't have to put effort into the game. It's a Liberty I'm owed as the team boot, I don't have to trail from one side of the pitch to the other.'

'You will not take liberties with me sir! That is not in the Rugby Union rule book.'

Dynevor became indignant. 'And what rule number is it that says you have to put enough effort into the game?'

'You are insolent! You will see me after the game!' He blew hard but pointlessly on his whistle. His face inflated for a moment as he did.

Dynevor jogged away saying 'I think he really doesn't know who I am!'

'Halt!' Beesely shouted, so we did, in surprise. 'I know you by sight!' he hissed at him. 'I know you by name. I know you by reputation. But I plan to know you better, boy, than you have ever been known before.'

Very odd man. He later gave us a penalty under the opposition goal. Our captain called his troops around him to discuss a strategy for a tap-kick and run the ball over the line. Buddum, buddum, Beesely cantered up to us. 'You will kick for goal,' he said.

'Er, we rather thought we'd try and run it over, as a matter of fact.'

'You will kick for goal and square the match. You could lose if you don't!' He scampered irritably behind the posts, briskly swinging his whistle.

Our captain, a scholar more than a sportsman, said 'This is all faintly embarrassing, Dinky. Perhaps you better slot one over.' He pitched the ball at Dynevor who took it on the head, connected with his boot on its impact, and sliced it away in a legitimate drop kick to the corner flag. Those of the opposition on their feet were caught flat-footed. Dynevor chased, picked up, and touched down for an irritating but inventive try. The whistle blew three times.

'No! No! No! Take it again! Cut out the tomfoolery! Go back and take the kick properly Dynevor! At once! See me afterwards you boys! You boys who are laughing see me afterwards!'

When Dynevor took the kick again he hopped forward, both feet together. He launched a kick at the ball which missed entirely, both legs went up horizontal, and he landed, laughing, on the flat of his back. Others fell on the untouched ball, but they were laughing too.

That night the old fruit stood at his door which gave into the Long Chamber flexing his cane. 'Come here, Dynevor, let us get to know one another better.'

'Arple!' Dynevor cried in comic alarm, and hid behind his cubicle. 'Debopbop!'

Mr Beesely called him again, in a low, threatening voice. Suddenly there was the saloon bar silence you see in Westerns.

Delavera walked across the Long Chamber. 'That is not in the Liberties, sir. This is the Long Chamber,' he said quietly.

'I want to meet Dynevor on more intimate terms, Delavera. I intend to examine his character.' He tested the suppleness of his instrument in an unnecessary way.

But Delavera was firm with him. 'No sir. This is the Long Chamber. And this is a matter for the Ushers.'

There was a struggle on the step, Beesely flexed his will, and Delavera lifted his chin half an inch. Carnahan lounged behind. Beesely looked away. He couldn't win. If he had tried to push past, Carnahan would have put his head in the way and exploded it like a shrapnel bomb: boom! He was capable of anything in our defence.

Delavera looked serious. 'Dynevor, you've distressed the new man. You've created a situation. We'll have to do something, but what?'

How were the Ushers to resolve this diplomatic crisis? The Long Chamber considered the alternatives. These came out as the following:

1) painting Beesely's windows black so he wouldn't know it was morning.
2) running a firehose in through his larder window.
3) putting a python in his bath.
4) putting a parrot in his pants.
5) putting a leper in his linen basket.

Everyone had a suggestion. 'He really is appalling,' one said. 'The absurd bulk of him,' another put in. We had to do something, we couldn't let it rest there. 'He's such a clot,' we said happily as we manhandled the pig up his stairs.

Beesely was standing in his room with a piece of shelving plank. At his private devices, he made a faintly pathetic picture, as men do when they are alone in the evenings. When he saw the pig snouting round the door he made a sudden move and startled the animal. You should never startle a pig, particularly when it has been drinking heavily. The pig moved quickly for such a big animal. Its trotters twinkled, its jaws gaped (remember, it wasn't so long ago that his cousins had been razor-backing peasant spear carriers in the Massif Central). Beesely shoved the planking end-on into the chomping jaws. The pig ate it. Chomp! Chomp! Chomp! The wood split either side of the jaws, and the pig approached ever closer up the ramp.

I'd been wanting to do this for ages and was disappointed that the experience left me feeling slightly shabby. Getting soft, you notice. I blame myself.

Anyway, it was by this means that the Watch found our housemaster cowering on the top of a cupboard with a rictoid expression on his fleshy lips. He didn't try to come into the Long Chamber for a while after that.

Perhaps you feel sorry for him. We never did. We felt shabby for having invaded the privacy of self (you wouldn't want to poke your nose in there, even if invited), but he was such a very stupid man that you couldn't feel sorry for him for long. Here are three examples:

1) When the sleeve of our collegiate life had begun to unravel, he addressed the Corps: 'I do not expect you to take pride in the Corps, or your House, or your school,' he said. 'I expect you to take pride in your*selves*.' Pure folly. And worse than folly, it was selfishness of a high order. If you took pride in your Corps, or your House, or your school, you would necessarily take pride in yourself. And at that age it is very much easier to be proud of your school than it is to be proud of yourself, boys being what they are.

2) He continually spoke drivel. We hated that. 'You are inefficient! I cannot abide inefficiency!' he'd say. 'Life is too short for inefficiency!' Life is long enough to take a very great deal of inefficiency. What life is too short for is watching Captain Pugwash on the television. He had a clumsy, rather bullying way of conversation:

'Gonzago!' he said at dinner one night, in an imperative tone of voice.

We looked warily at each other, then at him. 'Sir?'

He closed his eyes wearily, then added as if by way of explanation: 'Murdered his brother in the orchard!'

'Er, excuse me. . . ?'

'Hamlet. Act IV. Scene iii.'

'Really, sir.'

'*The Mousetrap*!' he said irritably. '*The Mousetrap*!'

He was remarking on the quality of the after-dinner cheese we were eating. He was implying the cheese was fit only to be used as bait for mice. Drivel, you see.

3) When he found some boys smoking in a pipe a mixture of wild mushrooms, baked banana skins and cactus juices, he became very grave. He talked about drugs, and the devil, and his responsibility to the parents. Now, I like opium as well as the next man (opium, alas, doesn't like me) and though you would be better to leave it till later in life I would rather see the school smoking opium than cigarettes. He caused the boys to be expelled. I damned him for that. Expulsion was a cruel and unusual punishment. When corporal punishment was abolished, expulsion became the norm for serious offences. By abolishing the rod, he brought greater pain into school life.

Mr Beesely was a man without innocence or experience. Nor did he have any respect in him. We should have bagged him in a belfry-sack and broken his spirit. Failing that, we came to an accommodation by putting a pig in his room and daring him to complain. It worked well enough, for what it was, in spite of the taint it laid upon us. We settled down together in a sort of absent-minded harmony.

We were happy. Dynevor, Hog, myself. They annoyed me, it's true, but that was what I was good at. We were suited to one another's company.

Little did we know, all this was coming to an end. These were the last days of our freedom. The shades of the prison house walls, at first a smudge on the horizon, were coming at us in increasingly threatening detail. The nights were drawing in. Mr Beesely's star began to rise.

The effective working relationship was violently disrupted the following term. Then Beesely threw off his subjugation and reared up under the sponsorship of our new Master. This was Dr Kennedy.

He was a tall, good-looking man, in a Whitehall sort of way (well-kept hair, white hands). The public voice he used was quiet, but very relaxed. He wore his tie with a dangerously tight knot. He was obsessively discreet. You could tell everything you needed to know about him by the way he ran. *That's why he never did it*! Indeed, only two things were known directly about him:

1) He had been seen in the town wearing a short-sleeved sweater (you know the rule – never trust a man in a short-sleeved sweater).

2) He had been to Winchester. Wykehamists are known to be mad. It is a clever school, and those boys who are clever are maddened by their cleverness. Those that aren't clever are maddened by their lack of it. Dr Kennedy was, beneath his awesomely quiet exterior, quite squealing with lunacy; quite yodelling with it.

It was obvious to me from the first. When he addressed us from his first term pulpit he said something so mad we didn't understand it at first: 'I want each of you to think what this school is *for*. What is our purpose? What are we doing? And how will it affect those around us in Society? What are the consequences of our actions? I want each of you to think about that carefully.'

I thought about it with indignation. Still do. Don't care how foolish it makes me look. I will splutter and go red. You don't ask what a product of nature is *for*. What's an oak tree *for*? There are oak trees. They came that way. And you don't ask that about institutions of Society. They came that way. They're a living part of the whole history of a Society. Therefore they haven't got a purpose. They are part of us. What is it *for*! 'Think what it's *for*!' What's the House of Lords *for*? Nobody asks that, and why should they? It is part of our lives.

As we know, we had little experience of abstract thought. As a result, we didn't have the mental equipment to recognise Dr Kennedy's intentions. They were so big they were invisible. Aborigines, I'm told, couldn't see Captain Cook's four-masted sailing ship as it first came into Sydney harbour: they hadn't the cultural equipment to see anything so large. Neither had we.

Now, I am not a man who understands matters. The things in my life that I have understood (my dogs, a horse I had, how to make a bed) have been rewarding. Fortifying, even. The things I haven't understood have made such a masterpiece of confusion that even a subscription to the *Spectator* hasn't been able to clear it up.

Thus, without benefit of understanding, my explanation is a complex one. Doctor Kennedy had been a prodigy at Winchester. He found admiration rewarding. Fortifying even. He deployed all his resources into the development of his mind. And that organ became powerful and restless. During the process, ambition seized and abandoned colonies of his heart and soul. And so he fell under the despotic power of a tyrannical dictator, and was driven to excess of conquest, with whatever scorched earth and broken walls behind him.

Not a weak man, in sum, but essentially bad.

And the demons he let loose on us! The demons he let loose would take years to get back in their bottles. Hog! He was *thinking*, and on Dr Kennedy's direct instructions!

The system is repressing our individuality!

'You just use people,' Hog told me angrily. 'You're an exploiter. You exploit everyone. You exploit me. You exploit the system. You exploit the workers. You exploit your colonies. You exploit the whole of the Third World. You people are so twisted you even exploit yourselves!'

'Obble-op,' Dynevor added.

I looked 'exploit' up in the dictionary. From the Latin root *explicitare.* To enjoy. Probably 'to take pleasure out of'. I confessed to it. I enjoyed Hog, tugs, Scullies, townsmen, workers, colonials and the broad mass of sub-continentals. I reached for a muffin, content in myself. A bell sounded across our view of parapets and spires. A late sun broke cover and the old stone glowed. A dazzling filigree around an ornamental window caught the light, the tracery came alive with a breathtaking glamour.

'The *squalor* that ordinary people live in is a total denial of any pretence of a civilised society.'

'Squalor. What? No curtains and things? If you want to talk squalor, my father lived for a month in a water buffalo!'

'Candy, you are a very, very stupid person, okay? Before we go any further can we establish that and agree on it, okay? You are an unthinking and, more importantly perhaps, a very *unfeeling* person. Are we agreed?'

'Agreed,' I said.

'Your father – possibly as dim as you are – killed a water buffalo and used its body warmth to survive. And therefore *you* say *you* know what *squalor* is. *You* know what it's like to live a life totally deprived of basic human rights. You have *no idea* what it *is* to be deprived of *all human rights*.'

'Do you remember, Hog, the first night you walked into the Long Chamber? The first time you saw those bare floors, and bare walls, and your thin little mattress? And you were put into The Pit? That's when you knew what it was like being deprived of all human rights. Hog, *you know what squalor is*. That, to my mind, is the value of a public school education.'

And then the conversation would encircle itself, I being unthinking, and unfeeling. Hog would make the point that proletarian squalor was different from public school squalor (we had a lively expectation of being promoted), and I would ask whose fault that was, and he would say it was mine, and I blamed myself and moved the talk around to the rucking abilities of our contemporaries.

In later life we ask the question 'Whose fault is it, and are public schools to blame?' And I say 'I don't know whose fault it is, but public schools are probably not to blame.' That's my answer.

'Public schools are the mechanism of how the bourgeoisie controls the proletariat breeding a self-perpetuating elite to subjugate the masses!' was Hog's answer.

I agreed.

Subjugating the masses is not a pleasant job, but *someone's got to do it*. You don't want the masses unsubjugated. We can agree on that, wear our hair how we will. The unsubjugated masses are an awful shower. Unsubjugated scaffolding workers: hands up, who wants that? We've got unsubjugated policemen and they're not even proletarian. How do you feel about them?

'To take pleasure *out of* is very revealing. The more you take out of them, the less you leave them with. Why don't you *just leave people alone*?'

It wasn't the way of our normal knockabout conversations. That was hurtful. I didn't like that.

The New Order

Dr Kennedy took a week to 'consult' every boy in the School, then he called us into Big School. I'd been 'consulted'. Didn't care for that. You weren't allowed to call him Master. He made you sit down in front of him. And you had to tell him what you thought the school was *for*. And then he interrupted you. 'Rugby football, Wynn-Candy. That's your game, I know. I also know you have a certain dogged talent for it. Let me say this. I am going to make Salisbury College the home of schools football. I can tell you that we are negotiating even as we speak to bring in one of England's finest internationals to coach the XV.'

That was his trick. The scholarly got his plans for science laboratories, the artistic got pottery kilns, the theatrical got theatres, the radicals got revolution. The thinking elements of College thought him a soft-headed smoothie who was trying to ingratiate himself with popular opinion. Quite wrong of them. 'They can't see how dangerous he is. He's a walking death trap.'

'That's what I like about him,' Hog said. 'Clearly a very able man. The only question in my mind is: has he go it in him to purge the old order? That's what revolutionaries must do right away.'

He purged the old order later. But I knew he was a bad hat very early. You could tell he was wrong by observing whose heads in the school went down, and whose went up. The porcine features of our Housemaster went aloft at a revolting lick.

The beast actually opened the door of the Long Chamber, and stood there. He didn't come in, he just stood there, boastfully filling the doorframe. 'The Master asks me to inform you that you are all to present yourselves in Big School tomorrow morning after Morning Service. This takes precedence over the normal timetable. You will find that things are to be different. Very different indeed.' As if to dramatise for us that he knew more than he was saying he insulted us in front of our thousand generations. He stepped into the Long Chamber.

Luckily a bomb went off in his apartment, and he left us.

'Did you like my bomb?' Rowse asked round my door.

'Very, very funny indeed,' I told him happily. 'I hear it was an offal bomb. Very, *very* funny, and very timely. He was walking through the Long Chamber when it went off!'

'Ha ha! I heard about that!'

'Offal everywhere!'

'Ha ha!'

We were happy, and is that a crime? How many of us can say that now, in our maturity? Now that an offal bomb, and Gentleman's Relish, are insufficient motives for happiness? We were young and strong and full of promise.

In Big School we sat like one great animal with five hundred heads. We were arranged in a semicircle of seats raked up to the ceiling. Dr Kennedy came into the room and walked up to the lectern.

'Yesterday a Housemaster's apartment was vandalised by a home-made explosive devise. Fortunately no-one was hurt.' He looked at us. The school did not move. The doctor had an impressive presence. 'I asked you earlier to consider the school, and to think seriously about what it was for. I must tell you now that I have been considering the school, while going through its records. I am going to tell you what I have found.' His bowed head came up, but his voice remained low. 'I have found a school that has performed increasingly poorly year by year since the War. A school that has achieved fewer and fewer university places year by year since the War. A school whose sporting record has disintegrated. A school in which discipline has been taken into the hands of a mob, and events are tolerated that should, rightfully, be prosecuted under the Common Law. I find a school in which boys paint their faces, and fight with one another like savages. I find a school that has lost its sense of itself. Subscriptions to the school have fallen and continue to fall. In two years time there may not even be a Salisbury College. And why? Because it is a school that is educationally sub-normal, a breeding ground of mutual servility, and a nursery of vicious practice. Salisbury College is the laughing stock of the Headmasters' Conference. I repeat, laughing stock.'

We wished he wouldn't repeat it. We were one of those extraordinary schools that could laugh at itself, but we hated it like poison when others laughed at us. Because Dr Kennedy was insane he had the apparatus to divine this hidden weakness of ours. Clever lunatics are unnaturally cunning. They can see through walls. They know without being told what you hate most, however you hide it.

'All this will change. It will change immediately. Salisbury College is to take its place in the modern world. We will no longer tolerate the pseudo-medievalism of an exhausted culture. After lengthy discussions with the Housemasters, the assistant masters, and Praesidium, and with individual consultation of every boy in the school, the following announcements are to be made:

'Firstly. Following sustained abuse by boys, all prefects have their beating privileges withdrawn as from this moment.

'Secondly. Fagging will be discontinued as from this moment.

'Thirdly. No junior shall be "taken up" by senior boys. Anyone found wearing or passing "pins" will suffer severe punishment. Any discovery of immorality will meet with severe punishment.

'Fourth. The practice of shirking will cease immediately.

'Fifth. Beer, including small beer, is, with immediate effect, banned.

'Six. Attendance at XV matches on Saturday afternoons is compulsory.
'Seven. Fighting will be treated as a serious infringement of school discipline and will draw a severe punishment.
'Eight. Silence will be observed during Chapel except to participate in the service in the passages provided for in the prayerbook.
'Nine. Any assault on any boy, any member of staff, or on any individual from the town will meet with severe punishment.
'Ten. Boys will not be allowed to walk alone out of sight of the school authorities.'

As a series of body blows this was a comprehensive pounding. So shocking was it that the beast which was College did not rise up like the Roman Senate on the Ides of March and perforate our Master with our dip pens.

His next move nipped any sense of rebellion in the bud. 'I have referred to severe punishment. Now I will show what I mean by that. The boy who caused the explosion yesterday, stand up.' No-one moved in Big School. 'Stand up, the boy who caused the explosion,' he repeated. Stillness. Silence. Then he said 'Rowse, stand up.'

I saw my friend adjust his cuff by shaking his wrist; then he stood up. The Doctor glanced at him indifferently as he said: 'Rowse, your offence has been reported to the police. I believe you will be charged and tried in a district court: it is of no interest to this institution. Leave Big School immediately. Wait in your study. A car has been ordered for you to take you to the station. You are expelled Rowse, in disgrace and without a character.'

Rowse moved to the end of the pew and looked round Big School. He began to say something: 'Well, it looks as though—' but Dr Kennedy, without raising his voice, cut him off.

'You will say nothing. Mr Beesely will escort you to your study.'

And Beesely did. He was gone by the time we were dismissed. We never saw him again.

There is a sense of execution about expulsion. It is less

immediately painful than corporal punishment, but more like dying. To be put apart from the comfort of friends, and the familiarity of one's cell; to have all prospects shut off suddenly, and to go who knows where, alone and unprotected. It is an awful punishment for a boy. And for a Headmaster it is the coward's way out.

'I say to all of you: go to your Houses. Each House will be addressed by its Housemaster. You will listen carefully to them and follow their instructions and follow them in every particular. Remember this. We have a great task ahead of us. The world has changed outside these walls, and we are now to change with it. There may be some of you who feel you will not want to travel with us down this road. Some of you, addicted to the twisted servility of an old regime, may not be able to face the freedom of a modern education. For you will be required to think for yourselves, to work for others, and take your rightful place in Society. There will be those who will not be prepared to attempt the act of adjustment. So be it. They are free to go, and the sooner the better. Those that stay will find they are part of a new system: one that searches out the individual talents of its boys and makes the very best of them. A school that cares for the growth and development of its members. A school that pursues excellence with a sustained energy and conviction that will make it the finest public school in Britain! *That* is my undertaking to *you*!'

Not a weak man, you see. He had risked everything in his address. We might all have lobbed offal bombs at him from the raked seats (you can't expel everyone). We might have started a Zulu roll with our feet on the boards. We might simply have hissed him until Christmas. He risked his prestige and he won.

'Yes, I think he'll do. He's ruthless enough,' Hog said. 'He's suspended the constitution. He'll purge the old regime. He's got control of the broadcasting service. Now he'll put his secret service into action.'

'What secret service?'

'Oh, er, I don't know anything about that,' Robertshaw mumbled and moved on ahead of me.

Beesely was shirked in Welsh; two tugs instinctively ducked into a doorway as he approached. 'You boys! You are shirking! There is no more shirking! Hold up your heads!'

When he walked into the Long Chamber each step sounded like a hammer blow on our coffin lid. That after so many years, so many generations, it should come to this, with a man such as he.

What he said was this (you will laugh): 'An evil elephant has come into the school. Nobody saw it come in. It arrived bit by bit. But now it is here, and we are determined to get it out. It is the elephant of impurity.'

So, impurity was an elephant, was it? Bit by bit I was getting to grips with the concept of impurity. No walking in the woods, no mucking about at night, and now, keep away from elephants. Was it something to do with the nibbling tips of their trunks? What?

'We shall destroy this elephant. We shall be visiting the dormitory every night. We shall make inspections without warning. At any time of the day or night. Either myself, or those appointed by me who will report anything they see. Lights out is at ten o'clock. Everyone will be in bed. There will be a silence until Bells. If anyone is found out of their bed before six-thirty they will taste the same medicine that Rowse has.'

That was how Beesely breached the Long Chamber, and how he was able to walk in it every night where no master had walked before. It was also how the secret service was introduced into the school. We were watched. At work and play. Study doors were to be kept open if more than one boy was in the room. Masters were no longer able to hold individual confirmation classes with the door shut. It was impossible to walk with one other boy without a hideous construction being placed on it.

'It's essentially an egalitarian revolution,' Hog said. 'We're all to be significantly more equal than we were. And that increases the amount of justice in the system, and that must, by definition, be a giant step forward.'

'I don't like it.'

'Because you're on the losing side, of course you don't like it. You are now powerless. The old hierarchical system is smashed. Now we all have equal access to the Housemaster, we all have equal access to Dr Kennedy. *Of course* you don't like it. You don't have any more say in matters now than I do!'

'But you don't have any say in matters at all.'

'And neither do you, so get used to it!'

There was something vindictive in his manner. I couldn't understand why. Dr Kennedy was introducing what he called a rational system of education consonant with the requirements of the modern world. That's what he told Hog. What he told me was 'I want to make Salisbury the epitome of schools rugby. It is important for us all to make Salisbury the best!'

He thought I would like that, but he was wrong. For Salisbury to become the epitome of schools rugby, we would have to win all our matches. And that struck me as a futile, not to say disreputable, ambition. Why should we win all our matches? We'd have to practise to an almost unhealthy, no – to an actually unhealthy – extent to win all our matches.

'What do you think about Dr Kennedy and all, then Dynevor?' I asked in an attempt to defuse an increasingly bad-tempered discussion about sentencing policy for working class offenders.

'David is unsound on Dr Kennedy,' Hog put in. 'He does not have a vote in this.'

'Oh pop!' He snapped his fingers at Hog. 'It really doesn't bother me, Wynn-Candy,' he said. 'I am the sort of person, you see, that these sorts of things *don't* bother.'

'David would be pulling the drinks in a brothel in Saigon,' Hog said.

I said, 'What, pray, is a brothel?'

It took a year to make the changes that Dr Kennedy required. He expelled twenty five boys in the first month, and then two or three a month after that. He was absolute in his authority. The evil elephant he introduced into the school he brought in piece by piece. No-one saw it come in. Suddenly it was there. The rational system of education consonant with the requirements of the modern world.

The College Tarts were removed from their position behind the rood screen. A number of boys chosen apparently at random were placed there. Hog had a place there. That was odd. They sat unsmiling through services. Was it better than the giggling and gossiping? I no longer knew. Near Christmas, Half Quad was taken up by workmen. We were told the flagstones needed replacing. In the Hilary half we found it had been laid to grass, with flower beds, and enclosed with a metal fence. We weren't able to play the Half Quad game. The afternoon scrums that moiled around Corunna Corridor with the inflated bladder, they were abolished by Trinity. And then the Watch went to Trading Post and took the braziers away. Additional periods were put into our free afternoons: work, or silent reading. They took the ravens away, one by one. In a year they were all gone.

Were we to surrender without any sort of resistance? Bewleys developed a plan to sack Dr Kennedy's rooms. They charged out of their house with water bombs and packets of soot, and a pig they had got drunk. They ran straight into the arms of a dozen college servants, each of whom collared a boy, and sent the rest packing back to their quarters. The pig bit one of the boys and ran barking for freedom. The following day in Big School, Dr Kennedy expelled the twelve. A muted groan went up as one after the other they trooped out of Big School.

'This is awful. This really is appalling.'

'You would think so. It's all over, Candy.'

'But Hog, how did they *know* Bewleys was planning a sack? Those Watch were waiting for them.'

'Oh, er, I really couldn't say,' he said. 'And don't call me Hog.'

'*Don't call you Hog!* But – but—' I looked at him with pain. After all we had been through. How could I not call him Hog?

'No-one will call me Hog any more. Call me Denis.'

'*Denis?* Why?'

'Because that's my name, dammit! That's what I am called! Call me Denis or nothing at all!'

You see how the fabric of life was torn in every direction in the course of Dr Kennedy's ruthless administration. The buildings were the same, the windows looked out over the same quadrangles, but it was a different school. The Liberties were gone. The tugs sat an abbreviated test at the end of Governor's Grace. They had no sense of initiation, the mystery was ripped away. Fagging ceased. Now the tugs were ignored by their betters. They were left to their own direct seniors. They had no access to other levels of our society. They lived a thinner life, in two compressed dimensions. Nor did the tugs learn the sense of service that makes him a kind master. Their whole sense of kind shrivelled. They were left, in short, to go to hell in their own individual ways. And there was a television in college. Captain Pugwash on Sunday afternoons.

Dr Kennedy had deposed the Bloods, subjugated the Praesidium, abolished the autonomy of each of the Houses. We no longer dined in our Houses, we ate in the Great Hall. We served ourselves on what is now known as a cafeteria system. On Wednesdays, if you preferred not to join the corps, you did 'community service'. It was compulsory to watch XV matches on Saturday; organised cheering was prohibited. Hog was unable to accommodate that into his theory of egalitarian revolution.

In a year, Dr Kennedy had effectively smashed all local authority. Nothing was done without his knowledge, very little was done without his approval. By doing so he gained an almost papal access to each individual boy. We see in hindsight that his egalitarian revolution replaced local loyalties with one overwhelming, autocratic power, unfettered by precedent, uninhibited by tradition.

That took the ginger out of us. When Hog and Dynevor came to annoy me, there was no pleasure in it for any of us. The Hog had found out what the average wage for tin miners in Peru was. He had found out that asbestos workers in America got ill more frequently than they should. He found out the percentage of Britons living on the poverty line. And he told us what he knew in suffocating detail, cross-referenced with contemporary paperback thought.

And then new masters arrived each term, and they were very different too. There was one – suede-shod, knitted tie – who found me in battledress arguing the toss with a tug who refused to be drilled. 'What you're saying, Wynn-Candy,' the new master said, 'is that every order from a superior is sacrosanct?'

'I do. Yes.'

'Then put your rifle in your mouth and pull the trigger.'

'But that would blow the back of my head off, sir.'

'So there *are* some orders you would refuse to obey. Now we're getting somewhere.'

So I put the gun in my mouth, pulled the trigger, blew the back of my head off and died.

Ha ha, only joking, I didn't really. But you should have seen the expression on his face when I put the gun in my mouth and pulled the trigger.

The master took the opportunity to blackguard me to my Sergeant Major. 'This boy is not officer material, Sergeant Major. He put a gun into his mouth and pulled the trigger.'

'What did you do that for, corporal?' He asked me indignantly.

'I told him to, Sergeant Major,' the new master said.

'You told him to put a gun in his mouth and pull the trigger?'

The master made a gesture with his arm, laying down his palm in front of us. 'It was an exercise, Sergeant Major,' he said wearily, 'on the limits of military authority.'

'You told this boy *to put a gun in his mouth* and to *pull the trigger?*'

The master withdrew his arm, wrapped it round his body. 'It was an exercise, Sergeant Major, I've explained.'

'I don't tell boys to put rifle barrels in their mouth, sir,' the Sergeant Major said. 'Not as a joke.' Then he saluted, his focus dissolving into a thousand-mile stare. The new master felt himself disappearing. He faltered, stepped back and turned away. The thousand-mile stare was unreturnable. The Sergeant Major was small but he was full of matter. A higher specific gravity than ordinary people. He was in all respects but position superior to the officers of the new regime.

I remember that he dismissed Beesely once, on a Library Parade. That was an illuminating experience. Brigadier Beesely, as he was on Wednesdays, took to drilling the whole corps for ten minutes. Four hundred boys on parade. His constricted voice floated down the files of us, and as we heard his voice, we came to attention. The sound of feet coming together sounded like ragged small arms fire. Drill is boring and frustrating under these conditions, and bored boys will not mark time as they should. Then the Sergeant Major marched onto the ground. He marched like a sergeant major, you understand, so we were all aware of him the moment he wanted us to be. He dismissed Brigadier Beesely with one of his salutes. He wheeled on us. He shrieked an order. We didn't understand what it was, but his voice hit us individually, and at once. The sound of our heels coming to attention had the dense structure of a firing squad.

For ten minutes four hundred of us were intimate in a way we could be in no other way. Our heels bit into the blacktop in perfect time, and we were connected together at a profound level, a level unavailable to a rational system of education. We were connected not just to the man on our left and right, but to every other boy on the parade. Under the authority of his voice we were connected at the roots of our being. And yet we didn't understand a single word he said to us.

People still say they prefer to do the twist on dance floors, rather than the quickstep. And those that do the quickstep do it with an ironic expression on their sophisticated faces even though they are enjoying it more than twisting.

The Sergeant Major left shortly. He felt the times were against him. He became a security officer on a passenger liner.

The Hop Quad Dolly

This was the year the dolly was banned by Dr Kennedy. The straw guy blocked in Hop Quad every year in memory of the events of 1355 ('Havoc! Havac!') was banned from Hop Quad. It was the last link we had with our illuminating past.

'No dolly mun go dun 'ere,' Watch declared in his characteristic way. He folded his arms stoutly in front of him. The knuckles on his weatherbeaten fists stood out like conkers. 'Thon Doctor sezzo, and there it be.'

'But Watch!' we cried, shaking the dolly at him (a horn came off), 'we've done this every year for six hundred years!'

'Was a time it dunt be laid neither, happen three year afore the Lunnon fire. Prior three year, whole school aback with a Black Death, and no-one to lay the dolly, nor none to whack him neither. Now here's another time, and my Master's a must to obey.'

'And what about the sovereign you take for your office at the block?' we demanded.

'That sovereign is not in the way of office, but a reminder to the young masters in their waywardness that the sovereign do reign yes, but also rule at Salisbury.'

So we gave him a sovereign and considered the position. The reaction was swift and strong. 'There's no *need* to talk like that, Watch,' Dynevor told him crossly. 'It's pure affectation.'

'Mun, tha chucklehead.' Watch didn't mind.

We, however, took a different view. We did mind. We minded very much. The members of Lodge – the secret society of which I can say nothing – met in the place I can't describe, and took a decision I must not report.

Whether or not that decision had anything to do with what followed you must speculate about amongst yourselves. You did not hear it from me. I would never tell you. Rather would I cut my tongue out by the root, and eat it in a fricassee.

However, you must know, what happened was this. I took the dolly's place. I went down in the morning before Chapel, and in front of an admiring group of diehards, took my place over the Hop Quad Block.

'You always told me not to make myself conspicuous, Candy,' Dynevor said, 'and yet here you are, in a public quad with your arse in the air.'

I was not put off by his fledgling wit.

Everything went well for twenty minutes. Then there were footsteps approaching from behind. Then there was a voice. 'Well, Wynn-Candy?' A penetrating question. Dr Kennedy had interrogated for the army. This was his technique to make you babble.

'I'm taking the place of the dolly. You didn't say anything about anyone taking the place of the dolly, so the Lodge got together and thought we could keep the thing going by—'

'Please don't babble, Wynn-Candy. Tell me.' He wandered around the block, wrapped in his gown. 'For how many years has the Hop Quad Dolly been placed here.'

'Ever since I can remember, sir.'

'About three years then?'

'Hundreds of years, sir, since time immemorial.'

He smiled. I didn't like that. 'Before the Russian Revolution, in Moscow,' he said, 'there was a sentry duty that fell between four and five o'clock at a certain spot about forty feet into Red Square. Two soldiers stood guard there every afternoon between May and September. After the revolution, the new authorities asked the army what they were actually doing. They appeared to be guarding nothing. However, investigation revealed that there had once been a purpose to their duty. Seventy years before, a garden wall had once jutted out into the square. And on the spot where the soldiers stood, there had been a gate in the wall. And through this gate, at four o'clock, every afternoon between May and September, the Tsar's children went into the garden to play for an hour. The sentries were posted to guard the little children. The wall was demolished, the garden paved over, the children sent to play elsewhere. But the sentries continued to stand guard, year after year after year. For seventy years they were posted. Until the Russian Revolution rationalised the army.'

I had armoured myself with forethought against his sophisticated incisions. I replied with, I dare say, magnificent irony: 'Wasting their time, were they sir?'

'I think the point is the sentries believed they were following an ancient tradition going back to the time of the Khans, whereas it was really just out of one individual's memory span. About seventy years.'

He had come round the back and surprised me. I didn't like that either. 'I see, sir.'

'Do you, Wynn-Candy? So you want to take the place of the Hop Quad Dolly. I suppose I should expel you then.' He twirled the ends of his gown airily in his hands. 'I'll have to think. I'll send to you.'

The sun moved across the court. Sometimes it went in. A breeze picked up and died down. At the edge of my eyes I could see the steps of the Great Hall where Sheba's grandfather had stood in a circle of friends. Now as much as that time before did I need the magic of that secret room where I fell into the flecks of Dynevor's eyes, and everything was revealed to me. There was a bird somewhere in the ivy. Sometimes there were footsteps, but Hop Quad was out of the way. Largely there was silence. More than that time before, I needed magic.

Then there was someone running towards me. A familiar searing sound behind, and the sensation of a blow which lingered, developing into something I recognised as pain. Denis Robertshaw said 'There you are Wynn-Candy,' and handed me a note. 'That makes you look pretty silly.' He walked off back in the direction of the

Master's Lodge, swinging one of the College canes. It's true this was part of the ceremony, but to tell you the truth, it was a part I had forgotten.

I opened the note. It said 'On examination of the College records, it has been established that the practice of shirking was introduced into the college by the Right Reverend Mr R. F. Morris MA in 1923.'

The sun moved, the breeze shifted into another quarter. Bells rang in their mournful medieval way. My chest began to ache and my fingers needed exercise to prevent them seizing up. Perhaps an hour passed. A leaf was blown across the quad. Then there were steps behind, and again the rushing noise in the air. Good God! The first two aren't supposed to hurt! That hurt!

'Another message from the Doctor, Wynn-Candy,' Denis Robertshaw said, and handed me a note. 'You know what I think? I think he's really got your number.' The note said this. 'The John-Go-Down. John Bunt, errand boy 1870 to 1877, Watch 1877 to 1901, porter 1870 to 1906. From 1875 to 1877 he waited between six o'clock and seven o'clock for errands at the top of Hall steps. Prefects were notified for last orders by the words "John is going down now". When Bunt was promoted his position was not filled again.'

A drizzle began to fall. Twisting, I could see the slate sky above the Hop Quad buildings. It was obvious what the Doctor was trying to do. He was trying to tell me that all the ancient traditions of Salisbury were just made up in the last few years. Well, but the Beaker People. What about the Beaker People then, and the three stones knotted in a syntax of string? And England connected to the continent by a land bridge? Underneath me, where I was underneath, there were bones a thousand generations deep in the earth. What about them?

In windows there were boys, they didn't look down. They were eating doughnuts, but no-one brought me one. Solitude and physical restriction are dangerous for anyone, let alone the young. They encourage introspection, and that way madness lies. The day lay around me like a wasteland. It was a prospect of boredom interrupted by moments of pain. But then I have heard married women describe their whole lives like this, I shouldn't complain.

Hog had put on rubber-soled shoes so I was not prepared for the third swipe. This had an embarrassing consequence. The surprise caused a spastic release of certain infra-gluteal muscles, and this in turn caused an involuntary emission of intestinal gas. It was audible. When I say audible, I mean the sound echoed. In fact it bounced around Hop Quad like a champagne cork. A crow was startled and flew off the battlements. The pain of the stripe was less than the mortification of the result.

The note, when I could bear to read, said: 'On examination of the College records, we have established that the "Beaker People", ie the stones tied in a string, originated from a disjointed rosary discovered on a body below the water meadow in 1916. The police pathologist identified the body as belonging to a gypsy, Alice O'Grady. Cause of death: suicide. Date of death: 1912.'

Hun gun dun. I got up from the Hop Quad Block and walked uneasily across to the broad steps. A stream of boys flew through the doors and came pell mell down, gowns flowing in their slipstream.

In my study I took out my Cozens and laid them on the table. I drew out the Beaker People with the missing stone, and laid them beside. Suddenly they seemed poor things. A hank of string and a cloth pouch. I put my hands on the table and bent forward.

'Look here,' Dynevor said. He waved a brightly coloured paper at me. 'Teacher, in the Bash Street kids, has built a caning machine. That is Danny who is under it, and he's shouting "Ooyah"! Have you ever said "Ooyah"? Or is it only what grammar schoolboys say?'

I didn't reply.

'Never mind, old fellow,' Dynevor said. 'It doesn't matter, honestly. My family line was traced back 2,000 years. We found an idiot who wore trousers made of mud and a leek.'

'Wynn-Candy has a horror of the future. He refuses to look ahead.'

'Well, why shouldn't he? I refuse to look ahead myself.'

'But you live in the present. Wynn-Candy lives in the past. About seventy years ago. Pathetic really.'

The Harrow match

Playing for your school had a ring about it in those days. Like Captain of England used to sound. Though a Captain of England now ends his career in a high street sports supply shop in Kingston-upon-Thames, playing for your school in those days was the finest thing that could happen to a boy.

Our story finishes here, as things should end on a high note, playing for the school, in the greatest match for a generation against our old enemy, Harrow.

Harrow is a peculiar school, do you know Harrovians? Every school builds in a disability to their boys (that's what character means). Eton builds in a sort of moral insecurity. Winchester, a mental insecurity. Charterhouse, social insecurity. The list goes on.

Harrovians, however, have been trained to be morbidly preoccupied with money. In the matter of Harrow I speak from experience. At dinner some years ago I asked a young Harrovian what he was doing with himself. He said he was dealing in diamonds. Before I could turn away, he had a briefcase on the table, between the silver and the crystal, offering me a selection of carats at favourable discounts. The middleman (whoever *he* was) had been 'cut out'. Sensing that I was embarrassed by the briefcase on the dinner table he made me buy all the diamonds he had to get the case back on the floor. Harrow, you see.

Dr Kennedy gave us certain incentives to win the Harrow match. If we were to win we would be offered scholarships at Magdalen. If we were to lose, we would be expelled, the Colts would be thrashed, Dr Kennedy would call in the inspectors and dissolve the College. He would follow us all individually through our careers – no regiment would accept us, and we would be buried in unconsecrated ground. He required us to win the match at any cost. If the referee had been short-sighted we could have carried shillelaghs in the lineout with the Doctor's approval. We could have sub-contracted a razor-gang to help out in the scrum. We were to win or die.

We found out the reason for his ungentlemanly obsession. Not simply the gobbling insanity I have already mentioned. No, it was worse than that. Uglier, more insidious, and yet curiously trivial. At the bottom of his behaviour was money. He urgently wanted us to win – no matter how – because by winning, the school would have more money. He had noticed that when the XV won their matches, more people applied to send their boys to the school. More boys meant more money. More money meant more – I don't know – art classes, and theatres, and microphones. More of what have come to be known as 'facilities'. In order to pay for art classes and theatres and microphones, we had to win the Harrow match by whatever means we had.

The fearless Buxton had left the year before, and he'd been replaced in the school's affections by a new fullback. Carnahan had stayed on the extra year to captain the XV. He had grown, he was now built like a bullock, his thighs too big for conventional tailoring. A college hero. Six feet tall, he had the stopping power of a post office pillar box. He had a casual way of waiting for a tackle in which the school exulted. A three-quarter would break through the line and charge down the pitch. Carnahan would wait nonchalantly. When the fellow tried to jink around him, Carnahan jinked with him, turning sideways, putting his shoulder into the chap's chest. The man's forward velocity would abruptly stop; he would rise up from his feet and fall backwards to measure his length on the pitch. '*Wumph!*' college would cry. Carnahan would then pick the ball out of the fellow's stomach and charge directly ahead, running right over tackles until four or five dragged him down, one on each branch of his body. We loved him with a fierce, submissive pride.

This was the player that Dr Kennedy removed from his position. Carnahan was not an accomplished kicker. He could boot the ball a hundred yards, but it was as likely to go sideways. Or backwards. And this was not acceptable to the new order which demanded a ruthless uniformity in work. Kennedy had realised that points could be scored by exploiting penalties to kick at goal. He reasoned that if a team had a reliable place kicker, most matches could thus be won. We hadn't realised it ourselves because we didn't count penalty points. They weren't proper points, (tries were proper points), so we didn't count them. Kennedy had no such scruples; he had found a kicker that could kick goals from his own half.

Where had he found this technician? On one of those moody afternoons late in the year. Under a troubled sky, far up in the high fields. Some boys were kicking about, and laughing. Dr Kennedy and Mr Beesely (standing in for the Master's bulldog) were about their rounds.

The ragabouts were playing a kicking game up and down the pitch. Dynevor was playing the fool. He put up high kicks that bounced in a complicated way. He laughed and made foolish noises. He breathed on his fingernails in an ironic way and polished them on his chest ('Thank-you fans'). But to the Master's cold eye, there was a special something in Dynevor's action and he therefore demanded to see him work. Dynevor quite properly refused to perform to this order. He miskicked, booted it over his head and cried, 'Oh Clara!' But the Master was not deceived. He had the intellectual strength of ten lunatics; he could see with his twisted vision into the corkscrew of a boy's personality.

He made Mr Beesely go onto the pitch to kick against Dynevor. And at this opportunity the boy's eyes glowed (not a pretty sight). Beesely kicked down the pitch, Dynevor chipped it back precisely six inches above Beesely's reach. The tubby one stretched, and missed, and chased the tumbling ball back into his own half. Dynevor let him boot it back and then chipped it back six inches above Beesely's reach. This went on again and again. Beesely would not give up, he played with an increasingly strained appearance of good humour, and Dynevor toyed with him.

Eventually Beesely stood too close, not ten yards, with his hands energetically raised, as if blocking a basketball attempt. Dynevor placed the ball upright in the ground. He ran up to the ball. He kicked it seriously. The ball was not seen to move. It took Beesely directly in the front of his face, and the man went over backwards like an acrobat. He landed on his front, that's how far he went over backwards. He was dead to the world. X-rays revealed that the cartilage in his nose was turned to the consistency of wet spaghetti. Dynevor ambled up and looked at the lump of insensate flesh. '*Gonzago*!' he hissed. 'I'll lug the guts i' th'other room!' And then he placed the ball in the turf between the short Y of Beesely's legs, ran in a wide circle and kicked it sixty yards to goal. He smiled beatifically and clicked his fingers: 'Pop!' He was happy.

As indeed was the Master. He'd found a fullback who could kick goals from his own half.

'He has tackled. He brought down Carnahan in Cock House. The finest crash tackle ever seen on Big Side, I hear. He can kick quite extraordinarily well. He will win matches by his kicking. Dynevor's boot will be the single greatest agent in the revival of Salisbury College.'

'He can tackle, but he won't.'

'Then others will cover for him.'

And that is how it turned out. For the last match of the season, the all-important Harrow match, Carnahan was pulled out of the line and replaced by a boy whose closest approach to rugby had been to sit in the lap of the tight head prop and ruffle his hair. They put him in the scrum at Number Eight. On scrum-service! His duties included buckling the second row from behind, and racing back into the field to cover for Dynevor. The match would run him ragged.

The day was clear. The breeze was brisk. The last leaves of the year were snatched from the giant oak by Big Side. An excited crowd lined the field of play. Rumour had it that national newspapers had come down to cover the game. The immaculate turf with its lush cover of grass invited the headlong tackles of desperate players. It was a profoundly glamorous sight.

Harrow came out and fanned across the half way. They were a big side, we noticed. Heavyset. Rather loutish. Like cashiered cavalry officers. You wouldn't lend your horse to them, not if you were fond of the animal. You wouldn't want your sister dancing with these boys. Carnahan stepped up to shake their captain's hand. The Harrovian was slow to take up the gesture. That was a mark against him, I wondered if they'd report *that* in the *Daily Telegraph*.

Clock House struck the half hour, the whistle rang out, the ball lofted into the air, a great roar went up from College, and the match swung into action. Three hundred and fifty stone of fighting forwards locked into the embrace of the game.

The first thing we noticed in the scrum was that their front row forwards probably hadn't washed in the last twenty-four hours – they certainly hadn't shaved. They made a point of rubbing their stubble against our faces in the front row. Why did they do that? Apart from being distasteful, it hurt. We were getting whisker-burn, and that made us reluctant to pack down with them. Perhaps a razor-gang would have been useful after all.

The next thing we noticed was that they talked to each other in the lineout. 'Are you going to Aspinal's party on the twenty-eighth?' sort of thing. And 'Did you get your twenty quid down on Unlucky Lady after all?' and 'Do you think there are any pubs worth the name in this awful little town?' It was as if they were deliberately ignoring us. This had an effect on our morale. When they did refer directly to us it was only to say 'Oh *do* leave me alone,' while putting their elbow into your eye. They also spat on the pitch. A filthy habit. You had to be careful where you put your feet.

In an early scrum they held the ball in their second row and the hooker said, 'Let's just see if these oiks can push us off the ball for a moment, shall we?' We roared with rage and heaved (Carnahan put in such a shove as bent the second row like horsehoes). Our anger was ineffectual: Harrow merely snickered and said, 'Has anyone got any cigarettes?' Then one of them asked, 'Anyone got the time?' and they released the ball from the back of the scrum and their backs ran fifty yards down the pitch to score under the posts. 'If they stop the match at half time we could go over to my uncle's place for tea,' the scorer said to his fly-half, 'He's got a Bentley you know.'

Their fullback converted the try with such a kick as lost the ball. Dr Kennedy clapped savagely. 'Tackle Dynevor! You didn't even try!' we cried, some with angry tears in the eye.

'It's really not my forte. I did say, didn't I?'

'They said they were going to hold you down and kiss you,' Robertshaw said cuttingly.

'Who did?'

'The second row. Those ugly brutes with the scrum caps.' Indeed, the second row was ogling Dynevor as we spoke – one of them protruded his tongue and wiggled the tip in our direction. This wasn't how rugby football was meant to be played. Harrow were behaving like Australians. It put the spirit into us and we rose up against our enemy.

Dynevor restarted the game with an upswinging kick, lifting the ball very high in the air. So high that we had time to charge underneath it, and all arrived together, our scrum, their scrum, and the ball. Carnahan hit the boy who took the ball with his chest and he went down. 'Wumph!' College cried delightedly.

It was the start of Carnahan hitting form. He played a magnificent game. Scooping up the ball he made for the line, struggling through two tackles. Then three of them hit him in three directions at once: his legs went high and sideways, his middle went back and his torso jackknifed forward. Their captain kicked him in the head and hurt his foot by doing so. Carnahan was the first on his feet. He wore a crooked smile and tripled his game.

I remember he broke from the back of the scrum chasing the ball, charging down the passing line, eating the three-quarters. He took this one by the collar and flung him one-handedly behind, leaping onto the next in line. Fair but foul, fast and furious. Like some kind of racing demon. Their winger received the ball, and noting the circumstances (Carnahan's face featuring strongly in the same) he kicked the ball back across the field to land at the feet of the Harrow scrum. There was some by-play – a muffed pick-up, a stalled hand-off, a tentative grub kick, and then their forwards organised themselves into a rush, dribbling the ball down the field ten yards, twenty yards, bearing down on our shrinking full back.

Carnahan could not be everywhere at once. Dynevor back-pedalled, squealing, 'Stop them! Stop them!' as we tried in vain to fall on the ball. Then Carnahan showed himself to be everywhere at once. He had made half the length of the pitch and came into the play from behind Dynevor's shoulder. He ran full tilt at the scrum, picked up the ball without losing pace and tore through the Harrovians as if into beach surf. He tore, as it were, through the belly of the wave and emerged in open air on the other side going forward with his three-quarter line fanned out to his left moving in support. Deeply moving sight. Tears to the eyes. A warm touch deep in the bowels.

Carnahan made a hand-off and came into the centre, making contact with his brave line. Their fullback came rushing at him headlong and crashed into his chest in a desperate smothering tackle but Carnahan had released the ball the instant before and Cavendish was off, streaking down the centre to score under the posts. College threw its cap in the air and congratulated itself. The *Daily Telegraph* stabbed at the ground with its shooting stick in gruff applause. The spirit was with us. Harrow didn't like that. They stopped chatting to each other. They set their faces in an altogether different way. They spat on the ground in a stomach-turning manner, but we affected not to notice. We had more important work at hand.

The match developed into a running game the like of which had not been seen in England. The ball span down the line. Both fly-halves fed their three-quarters with accurate passes, or angled kicks into the winger's box twenty-five yards ahead: testing kicks into space. Sometimes Cavendish collected the ball on the wing: he ran with long powerful strides, very quickly (he'd lost weight, his affectation had dropped away in training). His changes of direction were baffling; he sent a minimum of three men the wrong way every time he got the ball. His chip kicks! He'd push the ball on the fullback's left-hand-side but confuse the fellow completely by running round his right-hand-side. His sidesteps! They leant against the line of play so hard that they doubled his momentum. He was, in certain situations, quite unstoppable. At each of his strides he had a ninety degree arc of space available to his next step.

Even the referee was carried away: when we'd travelled the length of the pitch three times in either direction without a stoppage, Harrow stood underneath a Gary Owen and fumbled the ball into an obvious knock-on and the referee cried '*Play on! Play on! Too good to stop!*' Dr Kennedy made a note in his book and the master was put on a train in his rugby clothes directly the match was over.

The scoreline developed equally between us. Their scrum was heavier, they took more possession. But our backs were up on theirs, and we managed more than not to smother them, or chase them into touch. When we failed, they scored, taken by the heels as they dived full-length in the corner. It was frequently Carnahan's tackle, he was everywhere at once all the time. Carnahan was filled with the spirit and they could not stop him twice going over the line in a thresh of sweat and mud and a spume of scrumbreath. College roared. Harrow spat.

Shrinking Dynevor was having a productive game. At every penalty he threw the ball over the crossbar, from here, from there, from everywhere on the pitch. He played the sort of game only he could play: standing well back out of the way, guarded like an Indian princess from the rough and tumble of the game, scoring more points than the XV had scored all season: 'Pop!' like that. Then one of their scrum-caps got him on the ground and kissed him.

'Oh! *Ugh!* How *dare* you! You dis*gust* me!'

'Oh stop complaining Dynevor,' we said, 'you were asking for it.'

'I'm getting *sick* of this! You're supposed to not let them get near! They were all over me with their revolting hands! They're not allowed to *touch* me! You're supposed to be protecting me! You said you would, and you're not even making the simplest effort!'

'Oh put a sock in it,' we said. 'If you don't like it, lump it.' And, 'If you can't take the heat get out of the kitchen.' That was our mistake. You shouldn't say things like these to fellows like him.

He loitered. He missed a penalty, hardly bothering to hide the fact he wasn't trying any more. Harrow leaned into our weakness without scruple.

The pressure on their line was intense. We locked arms and stamped our boots into the shoving-divots we'd dug. Our shorts, unable to contain the bulging muscle, burst. We made another two yards. They were buckling. Not chatting. No. Too busy buckling. We leaned and made another two yards. Then their scrum-half pulled a man out of the back by his legs and snatched the ball from him. He slung it out to their fly-half under the posts and he let rip a long, tumbling kick from one end of the pitch to the other.

Dynevor, sulking on his twenty-five was fifty yards away from the game, all by himself, and dangerously exposed. The pounding three-quarter line converged on him from both touchlines. Dynevor saw them coming for him, tongues out, fingers twitching and a nasty look in their faces. Running backwards he missed the collection once, and missed it again. And, yikes, suddenly they were in range, on all three sides of him, coralling him. Support was on its way, he could have fallen on the ball (it doesn't hurt after the first few kicks), he could have run into the opposition and held them the few vital seconds. But that was not his forte.

He ran back, towards his own line. He tried to swerve that way into touch but they were there, he tried to swing this way into the centre, but they wouldn't let him. You've seen a gazelle being hunted by wild dogs? Exactly. He kicked the ball in the direction he was running. It sliced off the side of his foot, it skittered over the try line, three of the chasing dogs dived on it. A great groan went up from College. It was a vital try, under the posts, eight minutes from full-time. They were ahead: we would have to score again under the posts, and at that end of the match we were running out of penetration.

'You gutless little worm, Dynevor,' they said to him.

'Oh that's charming!' he responded with asperity. 'My fault! Everything's suddenly *my* fault! I at least was there! Where were you! I don't see why I should play at all if you're going to be like that.

Then something worse – much worse than Dynevor's tantrum happened. A Harrovian calling for the ball ran head first into the posts and collapsed. Cavendish bent over him with a helpless smile, but a group of them Harrovians immediately formed, and pushed him aside. 'Keep your nigger hands to yourself!' their captain said. And as Cavendish apologised, another jeered in with, 'Look, the nigger's blushing! Have you ever seen a coon blush?'

These were words we had not heard at Salisbury. They sounded ugly. Damned ugly. Worse than anything you could say to a fellow, worse than things about his mother. It was true, we realised, that Cavendish came from the subcontinent (I'd always thought there was something different about him, *that's* what it was), but it wasn't something we'd ever remarked on.

That, I believe, is why Carnahan hit the Harrovian. Socked him so hard they had to pull his fist out of his face. So hard that the referee sent Carnahan off after the stretcher. The first man to be sent off in living memory. The *Daily Telegraph* wouldn't like that. The disgrace was suffocating. Our spirits evaporated. We were fourteen men. Thirteen if you didn't count Dynevor.

The rain descended, so did the standard of the game. Boots in the ruck. Elbows in the eye. Early tackles, late tackles, high tackles. Low tricks. Awful chat. And then you felt the pain of play. In the lungs, and legs. And when you went down with the ball they came down on you: shins across your ribs. The bruising came up on our bodies like summer thunderclouds in Oxfordshire. Harrow was demonstrating its character-flaw. And this was to our advantage, for a team that played like they did didn't deserve to win. *Ow*, that hurts when the ribs give. But character counts in the end, no matter the talent that is involved. Or, *shikes!*, the studs across the throat. They were a dirty team, and they didn't deserve to win.

They held their lead right up to the whistle. Then, moments before the end of play, a kick relieved their lines, a long way up the pitch to the half way. Dynevor stopped picking at the mud on his knees and reluctantly took possession. He looked around him. Thirty shattered players, wrecked men, soused in mud, fat lips, bedraggled socks hanging like bandages round exhausted ankles.

Dynevor moved forward with the ball. A Harrovian stumbled at him in a semi-conscious state. Dynevor put the heel of his hand in the Harrovian's face and pushed. The man went over backwards. Dynevor giggled, looked about himself, and then leapt forward (physically he was completely fresh). He made a long, running S down the field. Their scrum tried to wade after him, but they had no strength in the legs. At the twenty-five, Dynevor kicked ahead over the line of three-quarters. They turned wearily, in slow motion, as if in lava, but he was flitting through the line. He had the ball, we couldn't believe our eyes, Dynevor was in possession, running for the line! As if from an age away, from another dimension, College was cheering, cheering, throwing its hats in the air, turning to one another and hugging itself. Dynevor held the ball in front of his body and crossed the tryline in a graceful curve, heading under the posts! I hugged Cavendish!

Harrow fell on its knees with its face in its hands! The excitement of the crowd registered on MoD equipment thirty-eight miles away!

But Dynevor kept running. Beyond the posts, you see. And the cheering faded in our throats. He kept running through the scoring area. He crossed the dead ball line. Silence fell over the field. He ran off Big Side, he vaulted the fencing, he jogged to the road where a large black car was waiting. A woman in black was sitting inside. A man in uniform opened the back door. Dynevor got in, with the ball, and the car drove off. We heard later that they drove to Big Side at Harrow where Dynevor scored under the posts.

He never came back to school.

Postscript

Well, that was the end of my schooldays. I left shortly afterwards and went on to do whatever it was I did.

Looking back I wondered what it all meant. People – quite decent people started not going into the army. Instead, they started going into advertising. That can't have been right, surely?

When you asked these sharp suits what they thought they were doing, they said they were helping bring more choice to the public. As if the public wanted more choice. Who wants to choose between twenty-seven different forms of breakfast food? What's the point of that?

I blame women. Men don't want to choose between twenty-seven different forms of breakfast food. All that shopping. All that shampoo. Men eat porridge for breakfast and there's an end to it. *That's* the value of a public school education.

You may want to know what happened to those of us who were so young and strong and full of promise. If you are not able to deduce it from their running styles, I can spell it out for you.

Robertshaw became a local government housing officer for a while. Now he owns a street of warehouses in the City. He turned them into 'loft-style' apartments. He called his property company Hoxton Occidental Group. HOG. I liked that. After the company floated, he put all his money into gold and bought the rights to an emerging third world country for a green experiment.

Daisy went on to Cambridge and from there into the secret service. When he wanted a Bentley he sold a laser-guided weapons system to Romania to pay for it. A thrusting young interviewer asked him on television why he had done it. 'I should have thought that was perfectly obvious,' he said.

Rowse became the head of a chain of advertising agencies. He introduced many new chocolate bars for consumers to choose between.

Cavendish did well at the bar, though he didn't stay long. 'Face didn't fit,' he said as he boarded his plane to Lahore. 'Some sense of comedy always hangs round a foreigner in this country.' After he became the youngest High Court judge in the country, they trumped up charges against him back at home and sentenced him to death. They were unable to hang him (general feckless-ness rather than physical incompetence).

Carnahan woke up one morning and found himself working for a repertory theatre ('God, I must have been drunk last night,' he said.) He appeared in the pilot episode of an American serial about a detective who turned himself into domestic appliances to solve crimes. He is in some foreign field now, entertaining the troops. By throwing terrorists out of helicopters, people say, but I don't know.

Dr Kennedy went on to a successful career in educa-tional broadcasting, and later to chair an amazing number of government-funded cultural organisations. His emoluments have been calculated to run into seven figures.

Mr Beesely asked a new tug to put his hand in his (Beesely's) pocket 'to find the dolly'. After a number of years in Pentonville he started a very successful prep school in Surrey ('Stringent but benign discipline,' he says to parents).

Dynevor? I heard he became a guest for some years after leaving school. Staying in people's houses and amusing the owners. He was said to have lived in Saigon, pulling the drinks in a disreputable bar. He lives with a woman in a large house in the north east. Dynevor . . . Of the many things I think of when I think of David, I wonder how he ran over the try line at Harrow. Did he come in at an angle, swinging the hair out of his eyes? What was in his mind? Was it 'Pop!'? And were there starlings? And were they wheeling in the sky? These are some of the things you think of when you think of him . . . Perhaps that's the value of a public school education.